STORIES ON CASTE

Stories on CASTE

PREMCHAND

Edited with an Introduction by
M. Asaduddin

Translated from Hindi and Urdu by
M. Asaduddin and others

PENGUIN
VIKING
An imprint of Penguin Random House

VIKING

USA | Canada | UK | Ireland | Australia
New Zealand | India | South Africa | China

Viking is part of the Penguin Random House group of companies
whose addresses can be found at global.penguinrandomhouse.com

Published by Penguin Random House India Pvt. Ltd
7th Floor, Infinity Tower C, DLF Cyber City,
Gurgaon 122 002, Haryana, India

Published in Viking by Penguin Random House India 2018

These stories were first published as *Premchand: The Complete Short Stories
Volumes 1-4* in Penguin Books 2017

Introduction copyright © M. Asaduddin 2018
The copyright for the English translation vests with the respective translators.

All rights reserved

10 9 8 7 6 5 4 3 2 1

This is a work of fiction. Names, characters, places and incidents are either the
product of the author's imagination or are used fictitiously and any resemblance to
any actual person, living or dead, events or locales is entirely coincidental.

ISBN 9780670091447

Typeset in Adobe Garamond Pro by Manipal Digital Systems, Manipal
Printed at Replika Press Pvt. Ltd, India

This book is sold subject to the condition that it shall not, by way of trade
or otherwise, be lent, resold, hired out, or otherwise circulated without the
publisher's prior consent in any form of binding or cover other than that in
which it is published and without a similar condition including this condition
being imposed on the subsequent purchaser.

www.penguin.co.in

Contents

Introduction vii

Thakur's Well 1
Salvation 6
Temple 17
One and a Quarter *Ser* of Wheat 28
The Woman Who Sold Grass 38
The Mantra 54
The Lashes of Good Fortune 76
From Both Sides 94
Witchcraft 112
A Dhobi's Honour 133

Notes 143
Note on Translators 147

Introduction

Premchand is generally regarded as the greatest writer in Urdu and Hindi both in terms of his popularity and the range and depth of his corpus. His enduring appeal cuts across class, caste and social groups. He was not only a creative writer in Urdu and Hindi, but fashioned modern prose in both and influenced several generations of writers. The fact that his works were published in more than two dozen Hindi and Urdu journals simultaneously attest to his extraordinary reach to a wide audience that formed his readership. Many of his readers encountered modern Urdu and Hindi novels and short stories, and indeed any literary form, for the first time through his writings. Premchand's unique contribution to the formation of a readership—and, in turn, to shaping the taste of that readership—is yet to be assessed fully. Few or none of his contemporaries in Urdu–Hindi have remained as relevant today as he is in the contexts of the Woman Question (*Stree Vimarsh*), Dalit Discourse (*Dalit Vimarsh*), Gandhian Nationalism, Hindu–Muslim relations and the current debates about the idea of an inclusive India.

Born Dhanpat Rai (1880–1936) in Lamhi, a few miles from Banaras, Premchand's childhood was spent in the countryside. Called 'Nawab' at home, his early schooling was in Urdu and Persian, much in the Kayastha tradition of the time. He also attended the mission school where he studied English along with other subjects. His father was a postal clerk who moved from place to place. When Premchand was only seven his mother died and his father remarried. His relationship with his stepmother was never cordial. He was married at an early age against his wish to a girl who was totally incompatible and he refused to live with her. His second marriage, to a young widow with literary interests, Shivrani, proved to be a happy one. When he was seventeen his father suddenly died and the responsibility of running the family fell on him. He was forced to discontinue his studies and take up the job of a school teacher. However, after his graduation in 1904 he became a sub-deputy inspector of schools, a job which required substantial travel which did not agree with his frail health. In 1921, he gave up government service at the call of Gandhi during the Non-Cooperation movement.

Premchand began writing in 1905 and contributed articles on literary and other subjects in the Urdu journal *Zamana*. His first short stories were also published in this journal. In fact, Premchand began his career as a short story writer with the publication of *Soz-e-Watan* (Lament for the Motherland, 1908), written under his pen name, Nawab Rai. The collection drew the attention of the colonial government because of its alleged radical intent. He was summoned, when he was on an inspection tour, to explain

Introduction

his position. This is how Premchand describes the situation in his own words:

> ... Those days I wrote under the name of Nawab Rai. I already had some information that the intelligence wing of the police was making inquiries to track down the author of the book. I could realize that they have found me out and I had been summoned to defend myself.
>
> The Saheb asked, 'Have you written this book?' I admitted that I had.
>
> The Saheb then asked me to explain the subject matter of each story, and finally burst out in anger, 'Your stories are full of sedition. Thank God that you are a servant of the British Empire. Had this happened during the Mughal rule both your hands would have been chopped off.'[1]

He was asked to burn all the copies of the book, and henceforth, get prior permission from the administration before sending any writing for publication. Petrified, he abided by the demands of the magistrate and submitted all available copies of the book to his office to be destroyed. Premchand realized that writing under the name Nawab Rai was no longer safe and sustainable, and to circumvent the iron hand of colonial censorship he had to assume a new pseudonym, which was Premchand. Thus, both Dhanpat Rai and Nawab Rai were

---

[1] 'Munshi Premchand ki Kahani Unki Zubani' in *Zamana* (Premchand Number), 1938. Reprinted by National Council for Promotion of Urdu Language, July 2002, p.54.

finally buried and Premchand was born, a name by which generations of readers would know him.

Themes

Caste

Premchand felt a deep affinity with the common man and his natural sympathy was towards the oppressed and deprived sections of society. No writer before him in Urdu or Hindi, and possibly other Indian literatures, had depicted the lives of the underdogs, the untouchables and the marginalized with such depth and empathy. Throughout his life 'Premchand did not let go of his unsentimental awareness of the grim realities of rural life, of life at the bottom of the economic scale' (Amrit Rai: 1982, ix). The oppressors and oppression came in many forms—they may have been priests or zamindars, lawyers or policemen or even doctors, all of whom held the society in their strangle-hold. Rituals pertaining to Hindu marriages and death were so exploitative and oppressive that these events were often robbed of their dignity and joy and spelt the ruin of families.

Premchand began his career by exposing the corruption of the Hindu priestly class in his novel *Asraar-e-Muavid* (Mysteries of the House of Worship, 1903–05), and then he continued the tirade in many of his stories. In the story 'Babaji's Feast' 'Babaji ka Bhog' he depicts the greed of the Brahmin baba who has no compunction in robbing a poor family of its meagre means, and in 'Funeral Feast' 'Mritak Bhoj' he showed how the predatory and parasitical Brahmins drive another Brahmin woman to destitution and her daughter to suicide. In a series of stories where the central character is Moteram, a Brahmin priest, Premchand exposes with rare courage the rapacity, the hollowness and hypocrisy of the Hindu priestly class, which earned him the ire and venom of a section of high-caste Hindus, even culminating in a law suit for defamation. But he remained undaunted and went on exposing many oppressive customs that were prevalent in society.

But his most trenchant critique was reserved for caste injustice whereby people at the lowest rung of the Hindu caste system were considered untouchables and were compelled to live a life of indignity and humiliation. The upper-caste Hindus treated them as worse than animals and this injustice was institutionalized through social sanction of the caste system. Stories such as 'The Well of the Thakur' 'Thakur ka Kuan', 'Salvation' 'Sadgati', 'Shroud' 'Kafan', 'Temple' 'Mandir', 'The Woman Who Sold Grass' 'Ghaaswali' and 'One and a Quarter Ser of Wheat' 'Sawa Ser Gehun' constitute a devastating indictment of the way the upper-caste Hindus have treated the Dalits for generations. The stories demonstrate that the Dalits were subjected to daily humiliation by members of the upper castes and this humiliation stemmed from the fact that Dalit inferiority had become embedded in the psyche of the members of the Hindu upper castes who had developed a vast repertoire of idioms, symbols and gestures of verbal and physical denigration of the Dalits over centuries. Grave injustice and inhuman treatment of the Dalits had become normalized, causing no revulsion against it in society. Despite criticism from some Dalit ideologues levelling some rather irresponsible charges against Premchand for depicting Dalits in a certain way, these stories—some of which have been rendered into films—have contributed significantly in raising awareness about the injustice perpetrated against the most vulnerable section of society.

Women

A considerable number of his stories deal with the plight of women. Premchand was deeply sensitive to the suffering of women in a patriarchal society where women had no agency and had to live their lives according to the whims and fancies of men on whom they had to depend—husbands, fathers, brothers or even close or distant male relatives. Women were expected to be docile, submissive and self-effacing, sacrificing their lives for the well-being of the family. Girls were treated as a curse to the family and their parents were subjected to all kinds of humiliations and indignities while arranging their marriage. Parents were sometimes compelled to marry off their nubile and very young daughters to old men just to unburden themselves of the responsibility and shame of being saddled with an unmarried daughter. The practices of *kanya vikray* (sale of a daughter in marriage), even *kanya vadh* (killing of a girl child) too were prevalent.

In his essays and editorials, Premchand made a strong plea for the abolition of the evil practices that made the life of women unbearable. He supported divorce in extreme circumstances, backed the wife's claim to half of the husband's property in case of divorce and inherit the property in case of the husband's death. He also wrote in favour of the Sarda Bill which aimed at raising the minimum age of marriage of girls. In a large number of stories, such as 'Tuliya' 'Devi',

'Sati', 'Goddess from Heaven' 'Swarg ki Devi', 'Return' 'Shanti', 'Godavari's Suicide' 'Saut', 'Thread of Love' 'Prem Sutra', 'Two Friends' 'Do Sakhiyaan', 'The Lunatic' 'Unmaad' and so on, he sheds light on the plight of women in an oppressive, patriarchal system. Through the immortal characters of old women like the Chachi in 'Holy Judges', the Old Aunt in the eponymous story and Bhungi in 'A Positive Change' 'Vidhwans', he shows how difficult life was for old women in a society that was known to respect its elderly members. The fate of widows, who were considered inauspicious and were expected to renounce all joys of life, was even worse, as shown in 'Compulsion' 'Nairashya Leela', 'The Condemned' 'Dhikkar' and 'A Widow with Sons' 'Betonwali Vidhva'.

The Village and the City

Premchand's love for the countryside is evident in his fictional and non-fictional writings. He has written several extremely evocative stories such as 'Panchayat', 'Do Bail', 'Idgah', 'Atma Ram', depicting the pristine village life of simplicity, honesty and quiet contentment. In fact, his fictional corpus, if read uncritically, would lend itself to an easy binary between country life and city life, one good and the other almost irredeemably evil. Yet, we have to recognize that he does not depict country life as an idyll shorn of all evils. There are stories such as 'A Positive Change' 'Vidhwans', 'A Home for an Orphan' 'Grihdaah' and 'The Road to Salvation' 'Mukti Marg' that de-romanticize and demystify village life and depict the author's awareness of the imperfections and blind spots in the supposed idyll. Thus, the apparent binary that

Animals

Premchand's deep interest in the simple life of peasants extended to his love for animals, particularly draught animals, treated most cruelly in India. Very few writers have depicted such an intimate bond between animals and human beings. Premchand depicts animals as endowed with emotions just as human beings are, responding to love and affection just as human beings do, and are fully deserving of human compassion. Often, the duplicity, cruelty and betrayal in the human world is contrasted with the unconditional love and loyalty displayed by animals towards their masters and those who care for them. It is a heart-wrenching moment, as shown in 'Money for Deliverance' 'Muktidhan' and 'Sacrifice' 'Qurbani' when a peasant has to part with his animals because of want and destitution. The deep compassion with which animal life has been depicted in 'Holy Judges' 'Panchayat' 'Reincarnation' 'Purva Sanskar' 'The Story of Two Bullocks' 'Do Bailon ki Katha' and 'The Roaming Monkey' 'Salilani Bandar' are treasures of world literature. Stories such as 'Turf War' 'Adhikar Chinta' and 'Defending One's Liberty' 'Swatt Raksha', written in a humorous and symbolic vein, show how a dog fiercely protects his turf and how a horse defeats all the machinations of human beings to make him work on a Sunday which is his day of rest, rightfully earned after working for six days of the week! In 'The Roaming Monkey', the author shows how a monkey earns money by showing tricks of different kinds and thus looks after the wife of his owner, nurtures her and brings her back from the brink of lunacy. In 'The Price of Milk' 'Doodh ki Qeemat' we have the spectacle of goats feeding a baby with milk from their own udders, thereby saving its life.

Premchand's Style

The atmosphere of dastaan and historical romances hangs heavy on Premchand's early stories. But he soon grew out of that phase and made his work more socially relevant by giving it the hard, gritty texture of realism. His art of storytelling became a vehicle for his socially engaged agenda of social reform and ameliorating the condition of the deprived and oppressed sections of society. However, that does not mean he was mainly concerned with the content and external circumstances of his characters and not with their inner worlds. Like all great writers, he took interest in unravelling the mental processes of his characters and the psychological motivations of their actions. As he says:

> My stories are usually based on some observations or personal experience. I try to introduce some dramatic elements in them. I do not write stories merely to describe an event. I try to express some philosophical/emotional reality through them. As long as I do not find any such basis I cannot put my pen to paper. When this is settled, I conceive characters. Sometimes, studying history brings some plots to mind. An event does not form a story, as long as it does not express a psychological view of reality.[2]

---

[2] 'Premchand ki Afsana Nigari', *Zamana*: Premchand Issue, February 1938; rpt. National Council for Promotion of Urdu (New Delhi, 2002), p. 173.

In the stories he has written one finds different modes and points of view, which he adopted by employing an array of narrative devices. An overwhelming number of his stories are written in the third person or omniscient narrative mode and a far lesser number in the first person. He makes extensive use of dialogue, using different registers of Urdu and Hindi in addition to dialects, colloquialisms, idioms and speech patterns specific to a caste, class or community. He also uses the technique of interior monologue and multiple points of view in quite a few stories. The salient point is that even though Premchand was mainly concerned with the content of his stories, to the extent of sometimes making them formulaic and predictable, he certainly did engage with the stylistic aspects too. And in this respect, he was influenced by both Indian—specifically Bengali—and foreign writers.

M. Asaduddin

Thakur's Well

1

The moment Jokhu put the lota to his lips, the water smelled foul. He asked Gangi, 'What sort of water is this! It stinks so much. My throat is burning and you give me water that stinks.'

Gangi fetched water every evening. The well was far off; it wasn't easy to go time and again. The day before when she had fetched water, there had been no smell in it. How come this stink today? She sniffed the water. It really was stinking. Some animal must have fallen into the well and died. But where would she get water from now?

There was the Thakur's well, but would anyone let her even step on to it? People would shout at her and shoo her away. The Sahuji's well was at the other end of the village but even there they wouldn't allow her to draw water. There was no other well in the village.

Jokhu had been ailing for quite some time. He lay there for a while, controlling his thirst, and then said, 'I'm so thirsty I can't stand it. Bring me some water, I'll hold my breath and drink a little.'

But Gangi didn't give him the foul water. She knew that it would make him worse. She did not know that boiling the water would make it safe. She said, 'How can you drink this water? Who knows what kind of beast has died in the well? I'll go and get some fresh water.'

Surprised, Jokhu stared at her. 'From where will you get the water?'

'What about the two wells of the Thakur and the Sahu? Won't they let me fill just one lota?'

'You'll only get your hands and feet broken. Nothing will come of it. Leave it. The Brahmin will curse you, the Thakur will beat you with a stick and the Sahu will charge five for one. Who understands the pain of the poor? Even if we die no one bothers to look in at our door, let alone lend a shoulder to carry the dead. You think they'll let us draw water from their well?'

This was the bitter truth. What could Gangi say! Yet she didn't give Jokhu the water.

2

It was nine o'clock at night. The exhausted workers had gone to sleep. Only a few idlers lingered near the Thakur's doorstep, chatting. Gone were the times and occasions for physical valour. Now there was only talk of legal prowess. How smartly the Thakur had bribed the inspector in a case and come out clean! How very cleverly he had got a copy of a landmark judgement, even after both the clerk and the administrator had said that it could not be attained. Somebody wanted fifty for it, some a hundred. But he had acquired a copy without spending a single paisa! One had to know the ways of the world.

Just then, Gangi reached the well to draw water.

A flicker of light fell on the well. Gangi hid behind the stone platform, awaiting the right moment. The entire village drank the water of this well. No one was forbidden except for these unfortunates.

Gangi's rebellious heart struck against the traditional restrictions and taboos. Why are they high and we low? Just because they wear a sacred thread around their neck! Each one is more crooked than the other! They are the ones who commit thefts and fraud and file false cases. Only the other day this Thakur stole a sheep from a poor shepherd, slaughtered and devoured it. Gambling goes on round the year in Panditji's house. And Sahuji adulterates ghee with oil and sells it. They make you do the work but when it comes to wages, every paisa hurts them. How are they any better than us? True, they are better at praising themselves. We don't go from street to street, proclaiming our worth: 'We are superior! We are superior!' If I happen to come to the village they eye me with lust, their heart burns with malice and yet they think that they're superior!

There was a sound of someone's footsteps approaching the well. Gangi's heart started beating fast. If they saw her, the heavens would fall! They'd give her an awful beating.

She picked up the jar and rope and, stooping, quickly moved away and stood under the dark shadows of a tree. Do these people ever feel sorry for others? They thrashed poor Manghu so hard just because he refused to work for them without wages. He kept spitting out blood for months afterwards. And yet they think they're superior to others!

Two women had come to draw water and were talking to each other.

'The moment they sit down for food, they order us to get fresh water. No money for an additional jar.'

'Our few moments of leisure make these men jealous.'

'Yes, it wouldn't occur to them to pick up the jar and fetch the water themselves. They merely order us to get the fresh water as if we're slaves.'

'If we aren't slaves then what are we? Don't you get your food and clothes from them? Somehow or the other you also manage to get ten or five rupees. In what way are slaves any different?'

'Don't embarrass me, sister! How I long for a moment's rest! Had I worked as hard as this in anyone else's house, I'd have been better off. On top of that they'd have been grateful. Here one may die of working far too much and yet no one has the decency to speak a kind word.'

Once they had filled their jars and left, Gangi stepped out of the shadows and walked up to the well. The idlers had left by then. The Thakur was ready to lock the door and go to sleep in the courtyard. Gangi heaved a sigh of relief. The coast was clear. Even the legendary prince of bygone times who had gone to steal holy water from the gods had not taken as much care and precaution as she was taking.

Softly, Gangi climbed up to the platform of the well. She had never before experienced such a feeling of triumph.

She tied the knot around the jar and quickly looked around, much like a soldier trying to bore a hole into the wall of the enemy's fort. If caught now, there would be no room for forgiveness or leniency. At last, praying to the gods, she braced herself and lowered the jar into the well.

The pitcher disappeared into the well gently. Not a sound. Quickly Gangi drew up the rope. The jar came up to the mouth of the well. Not even a well-built wrestler could have pulled it faster.

As Gangi bent to retrieve the jar and place it on the platform, the Thakur's door opened all of a sudden. Not even the mouth of a lion could be more terrifying.

The rope slipped from Gangi's hand. The pitcher fell with a loud splash into the water below and for some moments the sound reverberated.

The Thakur advanced towards the well, crying out loudly, 'Who's that? Who's that?'

Gangi jumped from the platform and ran away as fast as she could.

When she reached home, she saw Jokhu with the pot to his lips, drinking the same foul water.

Translated from the Hindi by M. Asaduddin

Salvation

1

Dukhi, the cobbler, was sweeping the doorway. His wife, Jhuriya, was plastering the walls of the house with cow dung. Both had just finished their work when Jhuriya said, 'Go now and request Pandit Baba before he leaves.'

Dukhi said, 'Yes, I'm going. Where will we make him sit?'

'We'll find a string cot from somewhere, right? Get it from the *thakurain*.'

'Sometimes you can be very annoying! The Thakur's family will give us a string cot, indeed! They never give us even fire to light with, and you're talking of a string cot. If you go to the bathroom and ask for a mug of water, they won't give it. No one will give us a cot. They aren't like our cow-dung cakes, wood or chaff, that whoever wants them can take them. Let's wash our own small cot and use it. It's the summer season; by the time Baba arrives, it'll dry.'

'He won't sit on our small cot. Haven't you seen how he lives—such restrictions!'

Dukhi said somewhat anxiously, 'Yes, that's right. I'll make a plate with mahua leaves. That'll be all right. Even big people eat from leaf plates. They're pure. Give me the pole, I'll pluck some leaves.'

'I'll make the leaf plate, you go. But we still have to give him some offerings. Shall I place them on my plate?'

'Don't even think about it, or our entire effort will be wasted. Baba will throw away the plate. He has a short temper. When he is angry, he doesn't even spare his wife. Remember, how he beat up his son! The poor boy still goes around with broken arms. Give the offerings on the leaf plate, but you mustn't touch it. Go to the shop with Jhuri Gond's daughter to get all the material. See to it that there is a full tray of offerings. Take one *ser* of wheat flour, half ser of rice, 250 grams of dal, 125 grams of ghee, some salt and turmeric, and place four annas on one side of the plate. In case you don't find the Gond's daughter, get Bhurjin to go with you. You don't touch anything, or else it will be disastrous.

After giving instructions, Dukhi picked up his stick and a huge bundle of grass for Panditji and went to meet him. How could he go to him with a request empty-handed? But what more could he afford as a gift except a bundle of grass? Baba would be greatly displeased if he went to him empty-handed.

2

Pandit Ghasiram was a devout soul. Every morning, he began religious rituals as soon as he woke up. By eight o'clock, he'd be done with the ablutions, and embark upon the activities of daily life. He'd first prepare bhang, then make sandalwood paste and, standing before the mirror, he'd draw the tilak—two horizontal lines of the sandal paste with a round, red dot in between. Thereafter, he'd make circles on his chest and arms with the paste, take out the idols, bathe them, smear them with sandal paste, make offerings of flowers, do the *aarti* and ring the bells. By ten o'clock he'd finish his puja, strain the bhang and come out. By that time a couple of his disciples would already be waiting at his door. He'd get an immediate reward for his service to God. This was his means of livelihood.

Today, when he came out of his puja room, he saw the cobbler Dukhi waiting for him with a bundle of grass. The minute he saw him, Dukhi prostrated before him, and then stood up with folded hands. Seeing Panditji's resplendent face, his heart was filled with respect. What a divine figure! A short, rotund man with a bald head, puffy cheeks and a divine glow in his eyes! The red powder and sandalwood paste endowed him with a godlike aura. Seeing Dukhi, he said, 'How come you're here today, Dukhiya?'

With a bowed head, Dukhi replied, 'I'm getting my daughter engaged, Maharaj. I wanted to know about some auspicious moment. When will it suit you?'

Ghasi said, 'I'm not free today. No, I'll come in the evening.'

'Maharaj, if you could please make it earlier. Everything's ready. Where should I keep the grass?'

'Place it before the cow. Take a broom and sweep the doorway. This sitting room also has not been plastered with cow dung for some time. Do that too. Meanwhile, I'll have my meal. Then I'll take some rest and go with you. And yes, chop this piece of wood. Then there are four bundles of dried grass lying in the barn. Get them and keep them in the storehouse.

Dukhi immediately set to work. He swept the doorway and plastered the sitting room with cow dung. By then it was noon. Panditji went to have his meal. Dukhi had not eaten anything since morning. He felt the stab of hunger, but he didn't have anything to eat and his house was a mile away. If he went home to eat, then Panditji would get angry. Poor fellow! He suppressed his hunger and started chopping the wood. It was a hard trunk with a huge knot in the middle, on which many more like him had already tried their hand. But the trunk was still intact and could withstand many more such attempts. Dukhi was used to cutting grass and taking it to the market. He had no experience of chopping wood. He could cut the grass easily, but here, even though he hit the block with all his might, it made no dent on the wood. The axe bounced. Drenched in sweat and overcome by exhaustion, he sat for a while, panting, and then got up to strike again. His hands felt weak, his feet started trembling, he was unable to stand straight and he felt darkness descend before his eyes. He was dizzy, but he continued working. If only he could get a chillum and some tobacco, he could muster some energy. But where could he get a chillum and tobacco from? Only Brahmins lived in that area. *Brahmins do not smoke tobacco like we lowly people do.* Suddenly, he remembered that a Gond too lived in that village. He was sure to have tobacco and chillum. He immediately ran to his house. Well, his hard work paid off. The Gond gave him tobacco and a chillum, but there was no fire. Dukhi said, 'Don't worry, brother. I'll ask Panditji for some. They're still cooking.'

So saying, he left with the tobacco and a chillum. Standing before Panditji's doorway, he said aloud, 'Master, could I get some fire to light a chillum?'

Panditji was having his lunch. His wife asked, 'Who's this man asking for fire?'

'Oh, it's that fool Dukhiya, the cobbler. I told him to chop the wood. We do have fire, give it to him.'

His wife raised her eyebrows and said, 'You're so lost in books all the time that you've no sense of religion. Anyone can come to our house, be it a cobbler, a washerman or any other low-born man. It's more like an inn than a Hindu household. Tell him to go to the barber, or I'll scorch his face with the burning wood. How dare he ask for fire?'

Panditji tried to explain to her, 'If he has come inside the house, how does it matter? He has not touched anything. The earth is pure. Give him fire; after all, he's doing our work. If a woodcutter had been hired for the job, he'd have charged at least four annas for the same work.'

His wife roared, 'But why did he come inside the house?'

Panditji said in a resigned tone, 'It's his misfortune, what else!'

'All right, I'll give him fire, but if he dares to come inside the house again, I'll scorch his face.'

Dukhi heard this conversation. He now regretted visiting the pandit. *She's right—how could a cobbler come into a pandit's house? These people are very pure, that's why the world respects them. They aren't mere untouchables like us. I've grown up in this village, yet I didn't understand this!*

When Panditji's wife came out with the fire, he felt as though he had received a blessing from heaven. He folded his hands, touched his head to the ground and said, 'Mother, I've made a big mistake by entering the house. But it is a cobbler's sense! Had we not been so stupid, we wouldn't have been kicked around.'

Panditji's wife was holding the burning wood with tongs. Her face was covered in a veil. She threw the live fire towards Dukhi. A big spark fell on Dukhi's head. He quickly stepped back and started shaking his head. He said to himself: 'This is the punishment for polluting a holy Brahmin's sacred house.' How promptly God has punished him! This is why the world is so scared of pandits. People steal money, but never a Brahmin's. If they do, they'll be ruined; their body parts will begin to rot.

He came out, had his chillum and set to work. The sound of the axe hitting the trunk could be heard.

When the spark fell on Dukhi, the pandit's wife felt pity for him. When Panditji finished his meal, she asked, 'Should I give this cobbler something to eat? The poor fellow has been working for a long time. He must be hungry.'

Panditji gave the proposal some thought and asked, 'Is there any roti left?'

'Two or three must be left.'

'What use are two or three? He's a cobbler, he'll gobble up a lot of them, you'll need at least one ser of flour for that much.'

His wife covered her ears and said, 'Oh God! A ser of flour! Forget it!'

Panditji now said bravely, 'If there's some bran in the house, then mix it with flour and make two thick rotis for him. That'll fill his belly. Fine bread doesn't quench the hunger of these low-born people. They need coarse bread.'

His wife said, 'Leave it! Who's going to take all that trouble in this heat?'

3

Smoking had sent some energy into Dukhi's hands. For another half an hour, he continued to work the axe. After that, he sat down holding his head, completely exhausted.

Just then the Gond who had given him tobacco came there. He said, 'Why're you bent on killing yourself, old man? You won't be able to chop this knot. You're trying in vain.'

Dukhi wiped the sweat off his forehead said, 'I still have to carry a cart full of dried grass, brother.'

'Did you get something to eat? Or they know only how to get someone to work? Why don't you go and ask them?'

'What're you talking, Chikhuri? Can we digest a Brahmin's food?'

'You'll digest it all right. First, you should get some! He had his lunch, went off to sleep and ordered you to chop the wood. Even a landlord gives something to eat. Even a ruler gives some minimum wages when you're forced to work. He's worse than them all and yet pretends to be a holy man!'

'Softly, brother. If they hear, it'll be disastrous.'

Saying this, Dukhi took hold of the axe and began to strike the trunk once again. Chikhuri pitied him. He snatched the axe from Dukhi's hands and for around half an hour worked the axe with all his strength. But there wasn't even a single crack on the knot. Then he threw away the axe and left, saying, 'You won't be able to cut this, even if you give your life.'

Dukhi wondered why the knot was not giving way. *There isn't even a crack. How long can I go on hitting it without making any dent? There's a lot of work to be done at home, something or the other always crops up that requires one's presence. But what do they care? Well, let me go and carry the chaff. I'll tell him—Baba, I couldn't cut the wood today; I'll come tomorrow and finish the job.*

He picked up a basket and began to carry the chaff. The field was at least two furlongs away from there. Had he filled the basket to the brim, the work would have got over quickly. But who would've lifted it then? So, he carried the heap in small quantities. By the time he finished, it was already four o'clock. Panditji woke up. He washed his face and hands, shoved a paan into his mouth and came out. He saw Dukhi sleeping with the basket of chaff on his head. Raising his voice, he said, 'Hey, Dukhiya, so you're sleeping, eh! The wood is still intact! What have you been doing all this while? You spent the entire day to carry a fistful of chaff! On top of it, you're sleeping. Pick up the axe and split the trunk. You can't even chop a little piece of wood! And you expect me to pick an auspicious moment for you? Don't blame me. That is why it is said, the moment a lowly person gets enough to eat he becomes spoilt.'

Dukhi picked up the axe once again. He forgot what he had planned to say. He was starving. He had not eaten anything since morning. He found it difficult to stand up. His heart was sinking, but he reasoned with himself and strove on. *He's a pandit; if he doesn't think of an auspicious moment, then all will be ruined. That's why he is held in such esteem. Everything depends on the auspicious moment. It can make or break anyone's life.* Panditji came and stood near the knot and egged him on. 'Yes, hit it hard, hit it some more, hit harder, oh, hit it with some more power, don't you have any strength in your hands—hit it, why do you just keep standing there, wondering? Look, it's about to split! Hit in the crack!'

Dukhi was not in his senses. Some unknown power was making his hands work. As if all that fatigue, hunger, weakness had vanished. He was surprised at his own strength. Every stroke of the axe was like a thunderbolt. He kept on working in that frenzy for another half an hour. So much so that the piece of wood split and the axe fell from Dukhi's hands. Overpowered by hunger and thirst, his tired body gave way and he collapsed.

Panditji called out, 'Get up and strike it some more. Cut it into small pieces.' But Dukhi did not get up. Panditji did not think it right to trouble him any more. He went inside, bathed and came out wearing the pandit's habit. Dukhi was still lying down. Panditji called out loud, 'Will you just keep lying here, Dukhi? Come, let's go to your house. I hope you've got all the stuff ready?'

Dukhi still did not get up.

Now Panditji began to have some doubts. As he went close, he saw Dukhi's body lying stiff. Panicking, he ran back and told his wife, 'Dukhi seems to have died.'

His wife was shocked and said, 'Wasn't he cutting the wood right now?'

'Yes, he died while cutting the wood. What'll happen now?'

His wife said calmly, 'What will happen? Send word to the cobblers. Ask them to take the body away.'

In a moment, the news spread throughout the village where only one household belonged to the Gonds. The way to the well was where the corpse was lying. People stopped passing that way. Who would go to the well passing an untouchable's body? An old woman told Panditji, 'Why don't you get the corpse disposed of? How can the people of

Salvation

the village draw water from the well? Meanwhile, the Gonds went to the cobblers' enclosure and told them, 'Beware! Don't go pick up the corpse! The police will investigate first. Is it a joke to take a poor man's life? Even though he's a pandit, it doesn't mean he can do anything and get away with it.'

When the Panditji arrived there, the cobblers were adamant that they would not pick up the corpse. Yes, both Dukhi's wife and daughter came mourning to Panditji's house and began howling. There were also about a dozen low-caste women with them; some cried, some consoled. But there was no low-caste man. Panditji threatened them, coaxed them but they were scared of the police. No one budged. Ultimately, he went back inside the house, disappointed.

4

The crying and howling continued till midnight. It was difficult for even the gods to sleep. But no one came to pick the corpse up and how could a high-caste holy man pick up an untouchable's dead body? That's not written in any religious text. Has anyone seen such a thing happen?

The pandit's wife was annoyed. 'These witches are giving me a headache. Aren't they tired of howling?'

Panditji said, 'Let them cry as much as they want. When he was alive, no one had cared for him. Now that he's dead, everyone has come to create a ruckus.'

'But it's inauspicious.'

'Yes, highly inauspicious!'

'The stench has begun to spread already.'

'Wasn't he a cobbler! They eat everything, without discrimination.'

'Don't they feel any repulsion?'

'They're rotten—one and all.'

Somehow the night passed. In the morning too, no cobbler came. The women had left after their lamentation. The stench began to spread now.

Panditji took out a piece of rope. He made a noose with it and slipped it around the corpse's leg. Dawn was breaking. He caught the other end of the rope and started pulling the corpse, and took it outside the village. He returned immediately, took a bath, read the scriptures and sprinkled the holy water of the Ganga in his house.

Meanwhile, jackals and vultures, crows and dogs had pounced on Dukhi's body. This was the reward for a lifetime of devotion, service and allegiance.

Translated from the Hindi by M. Asaduddin

Temple

1

Salute to motherly love! Everything else in this world is false; indeed, all else is transitory, frail. For the past three days, Sukhiya had taken neither a morsel of food nor a drop of water. Lying on the straw, the mother's child was groaning. For the past three days he hadn't opened his eyes. Sometimes his mother would take him in her lap, sometimes she would make him sleep on the straw. Nobody could tell what had happened all of a sudden to such a lively child. In such a condition how could a mother feel hungry or thirsty? Once she had taken a sip of water but it would not go down her throat; the poor soul's trouble was boundless. She had already surrendered two of her children to the Ganga. Her husband was dead. Now this child was her sole reason to live. Oh! Did God want to snatch him away too? Tears streamed down her face as such thoughts came to her mind. She didn't leave the child alone even for a moment. She took him along when she went to cut grass, to the bazaar to sell the grass; she kept the child in her lap all the time. Sukhiya had got a small sickle and a tiny woven basket made for him. Jayawan would cut the grass with his mother and exclaim proudly, 'Mother, make me a big sickle, we will cut a lot of grass. You can sit at the door sill and rest, I will sell it in the market.' The mother would ask, 'Son, what will you bring for me?' Jayawan promised her bright red saris while he wanted a whole lot of jaggery for himself. These innocent words kept coming back to her and piercing her heart like an arrow. Whosoever saw the child said it was the effect of witchcraft. But whose spell? How could this widow have an enemy? If one had some clue as to who it was, Sukhiya would fall at his feet and keep the child in his lap. Wouldn't his heart melt? But nobody was telling her the name! Whom should she ask? What should she do?

2

Three hours of night had passed. Her worried and restless heart was wandering. Which goddess should I seek protection from? To which god should I make a vow? Lying in this condition she dozed off. She saw her husband standing by the child's bed and stroking his hair. He said to her, 'Don't weep Sukhiya! Your child will recover. Go and worship *thakurji* tomorrow, he will be your support.' Sukhiya's eyes opened. Her husband had definitely been there; Sukhiya had no doubt about it. The fact that he cared for her made her heart hopeful. Her eyes brimmed with tears of faith and love. She took the child in her lap and gazing towards the sky said, 'God! May my child recover, I will worship you, have mercy on this orphaned widow.'

Jayawan's eyes opened at that very moment. He asked for water. His mother rushed to fetch him water in a small bowl and made him drink.

After drinking the water, Jayawan said, 'Mother, is it day or night?'

Sukhiya replied, 'It is night, son. How do you feel?'

'I'm well, mother. Now I've recovered.'

'God bless you, my child, I will pray to God that you get well soon. Do you feel like eating something?'

'Yes, mother, give me some jaggery.'

'Don't eat jaggery, son. It will harm you. Should I make some khichdi for you?'

'No, mother! Give me a little jaggery, I fall at your feet.'

His mother could not ignore his plea. She took out a little jaggery and placed it in Jayawan's hand. As she was closing the lid of the jar, someone called from outside. She left the jar there and went to open the door. Jayawan took out two more lumps of jaggery and quickly ate them.

3

The whole day Jayawan was fine. He ate some khichdi, once or twice he also went to the door slowly, and in spite of being unable to play with his companions, his heart was amused seeing them play. Sukhiya thought her son had recovered. In one or two days when she had some money in hand she would go to worship thakurji. The winter day passed in sweeping, bathing, eating and drinking, but when in the evening Jayawan's health worsened, Sukhiya got worried. A suspicion arose in her heart that it was because of the delay in worship that her son had had a relapse. There was still some daytime left, so she made the child lie down and started gathering things for the puja. She got flowers from the zamindar's garden. The tulsi plant was at her doorstep. But she also needed some sweets to offer as bhog to thakurji. Else, what would she distribute among the villagers? She definitely needed at least an anna to offer thakurji. She scoured the entire village looking for a lender, but when she didn't get money from anywhere she grew sad. Bad days, nobody lends even four annas. At last she took off the silver bangles she was wearing and ran to the pawnbroker. She pawned them, bought sweets and ran to her house. When the things were arranged, she picked up the child in one hand, held the puja tray in the other and ran towards the temple.

The aarti bells were ringing in the temple. Five to ten devotees were standing and chanting hymns of praise to God. Meanwhile Sukhiya went and stood in front of the temple.

The priest asked, 'What's the matter? What are you doing here?'

Sukhiya moved closer to the platform and said, 'I had kept a vow for thakurji, Maharaj. So I have come to offer puja.'

In the daytime the priest worshipped his zamindar customers, in the morning and evening, thakurji's. He slept in the temple at night. His food was also cooked in the temple, as a consequence of which the statue of thakurji had blackened. He was very kind-hearted, and such a devotee that no matter how cold it grew, no matter how harsh the wind blew, he didn't even drink water without bathing. In spite of this if there was a layer of dirt on his hands and feet it wasn't his fault. He said, 'So, you want to come inside? The puja is over. Will you come and defile it?'

A devotee remarked, 'She has come to purify thakurji.'

Sukhiya said helplessly, 'I have come to touch the feet of thakurji, Sir. I have brought all the things required for the puja.'

The priest said, 'How do you talk so ignorantly? Have you gone mad? How will *you* touch thakurji?'

Till now Sukhiya had never had the opportunity to come to thakurji's door. Surprised she said, 'Sir! He is lord of the world. Even the sinners get redemption after visiting him. Will he get contaminated if I touch him?'

'Aren't you a *chamarin*?'

'So hasn't God created Chamars? Is there some other God for Chamars? I have kept a vow for this child, Sir!'

The devotee who had spoken earlier and was done with the prayers remarked angrily, 'Give the witch a good thrashing. She has come to destroy our faith. Throw away her puja tray. The world is already on fire. If the tanners also start worshipping thakurji will the earth remain as it is or go into the abyss?'

Another devotee said, 'Now poor thakurji will have to eat from a tanner's hand. Now we are really approaching doomsday.'

It was cold. Sukhiya stood shivering as the contractors of religion were debating on the times. The child clung to his mother's chest for warmth but Sukhiya showed no sign of budging from there. It seemed as if both her feet had grown roots. Every now and then a deep desire to fall at thakurji's feet would arise in her heart. Is he only *their* thakurji? Doesn't he have any relationship with the poor like us? Who are these people to stop me? But she feared that these people would really throw away her puja tray, and then what would she do?

So she repressed her emotions. Suddenly an idea struck her. She went and hid herself in the darkness in the shadow of a tree and waited for the devotees to depart.

4

After the aarti and prayers, the devotees read out the Bhagwat for a long time. On the other side the priest lit the fire and started cooking. He kept on saying 'hmm, hmm' while sitting in front of the fire, and from time to time he would make a suggestion. The reading went on till ten o'clock—Sukhiya was keeping an eye from beneath the tree.

At last the devotees started departing for their homes one by one. The priest was left alone. Sukhiya went and stood in front of the temple veranda. The priest was busy listening to melodious tunes while waiting eagerly for his food. The sound of light footsteps made the priest raise his head. He saw Sukhiya standing there. Irritated, he said, 'Why are you still standing here?' Placing the tray on the floor, Sukhiya pleaded most abjectly, 'Maharajji, I am very unfortunate. This child is the sole reason for my life. Have pity on me, he hasn't raised his head for three days. You will be highly blessed, Maharajji.'

Sukhiya started sobbing. The priest was kind-hearted. But how could he commit the grave sin of allowing a chamarin to touch thakurji. Who knew what punishment thakurji would give him for this! After all, he too had children. What if thakurji got angry and destroyed the entire village? He said, 'Go home and chant God's name, your child will recover. I am giving you basil leaves. Apply *charnamrita* on his eyes. God willing, everything will be all right.'

Sukhiya pleaded, 'Won't you let me fall at thakurji's feet, Maharajji? I am bereaved. I have borrowed money and brought the items needed for the puja. I had a dream yesterday in which I was asked to go and worship thakurji so my child can recover. I have money, take it from me and allow me for a moment to fall at thakurji's feet.'

This idea made the priest's faith dwindle a bit, but being illiterate, he still had God's fear in his heart. Gathering his wits he said, 'O mad woman! Does thakurji see the devotion in the heart of the devotees or who is falling at his feet? Haven't you heard the proverb—"If the mind is pure, then Ganga is close at hand." If one does not have devotion in the heart, no matter how many times one falls at his feet, it doesn't make any difference. I have an amulet, it is expensive but I will give it to you for only a rupee. Tie this around the child's neck, that's it. He will start playing from tomorrow.'

'So you will not let me worship thakurji?'

'This much worship is enough for you, which has never happened before. Suppose I perform the puja and some calamity falls on the village? Why don't you think about that? Take this prayer with you. God willing, the child will get relief from his pain tonight. Somebody has cast a spell on him. And little wonder, he is very lively and draws people's attention.'

'My life has been caught in a whirlpool since the day he fell ill.'

'He is a very talented boy, may God keep him alive. He will take away all your pain and suffering. He used to come here a lot to play. For the past two three days I have not been seeing him.'

'So how do I tie the amulet, Maharaj?'

'I am tying it in cloth and giving it to you, just tie it around his neck. At this hour where will you go looking for new cloth?'

Sukhiya had received two rupees for her silver bangles. One was already spent. She gave the second to the priest and taking the amulet returned home, consoling her heart.

5

The moment she reached home Sukhiya tied the amulet around the child's neck. But as the night grew, the child's fever increased. By three o'clock his hands and feet started getting cold. Worried, she started thinking, Oh! I was so stupid and selfish for not having fallen at thakurji's feet and returning home. If I had entered the temple and fallen at God's feet, what could anyone have done? They would have pushed me out of the temple—only that would have happened. Maybe they would have beaten me but my mission would have been accomplished. If I could have washed the feet of thakurji with my tears and placed the boy at his feet, wouldn't he have taken mercy on me? He is a merciful God, fulfils the wishes of orphans, wouldn't he have mercy on me? Sukhiya's heart grew restless. She must not delay. She would definitely go and fall at thakurji's feet and cry. The helpless woman's scared heart could see no other way. If the temple gates were closed she would break the lock. Has thakurji been sold to someone that he needs to be locked?

It was three o'clock at night. Sukhiya wrapped the child in a blanket and took him in her arms, and holding the tray in one hand walked towards the temple. The moment she stepped out of the house, the wave of chilly winds made her chest shiver. Her feet were growing numb from the cold. On top of that it was dark all around. The distance was no less than two furlongs. The path winded through the trees. At some distance, on the left, there was a pond. There was a bamboo hut nearby which was owned by a washerman who had died, and now it was a den for witches. On the left, there were lush green fields. There was silence all around, the darkness was gasping. Occasionally, jackals would howl, making a terrifying sound. Oh! Even if someone had offered her lakhs of rupees she wouldn't have come to this place. But motherly affection had overtaken all the fear of danger. 'O God! You are my sole hope.' Chanting this she walked towards the temple.

When she reached the temple door, she tried to figure out the lock, but it was chained shut. The priest was sleeping in the room adjacent to the veranda. There was darkness everywhere. Sukhiya picked up a brick beneath the platform and started hitting the lock hard. Her hands were filled with a strange power. After two or three attempts both the lock and the brick broke and fell on the floor. She was about to open the door and enter when the priest woke up, opened the door, came out and started shouting, 'Thief! Thief!' and then ran towards the village. In the winter, people woke up before dawn. When they heard the commotion many men came out from here and there with lanterns and asked, 'Where's the thief? Which way did he go?'

The priest said, 'The temple door is open. I heard some commotion.'

All of a sudden Sukhiya came out of the veranda to the platform and said, 'There is no thief, it's me, I had come to worship thakurji. I haven't yet entered and you people have already raised a ruckus.'

The priest howled, 'What a calamity! Sukhiya has entered the temple and rendered thakurji impure!'

As expected, many agitated men leapt at Sukhiya and started kicking and boxing her. Sukhiya was holding the child with one hand and protecting him with the other. Suddenly a strong Thakur pushed her hard and the child fell from her hands but he neither cried nor said anything. The child wasn't breathing and Sukhiya had fallen on the ground. When she gathered herself and picked up the child, her eyes fell on his face. It appeared as if it was a reflection in the water. She let out a shriek. She touched the forehead of her child and saw that his entire body was cold. She drew a long breath and stood up. There were no tears in her eyes, her face was blazing with anger, sparks rained from her eyes, both her hands were clenched into fists. She clenched her teeth and said, 'Sinners, why are you standing away after taking my child's life? Why don't you kill me too? On my touch thakurji will become untouchable. On coming into contact with a touchstone, iron turns to gold; the touchstone doesn't turn into iron. Didn't thakurji become impure while making me? So, I will never touch thakurji now. Keep him locked safe, set up guards. Oh! You merciless people! You are so hard-hearted! In spite of having children you didn't have mercy on this unfortunate mother; on top of it, you have become the contractors of religion. All of you are murderers! The perfect murderers! Don't be afraid. I won't go to the police station; my justice will be done by God. Now I will plead in His court.'

Nobody uttered a word, nobody stirred. All of them stood with their heads bowed low, like statues made of stone.

The entire village gathered at the scene. Sukhiya looked at the child once again, and a cry escaped her mouth, 'Oh! My darling!' Then she fainted and fell on the ground, and her soul left her body. The mother had sacrificed her life for the child.

Mother, you are blessed. The devotion you have, the loyalty you possess, is difficult to find even among the gods.

Translated from the Urdu by Shaheen Saba

One and a Quarter *Ser* of Wheat

1

There was a village where a peasant named Shankar lived. He was simple, honest and poor. He was a straightforward person and did not interfere in anyone's affairs. He did not know how to manipulate, and never took recourse to duplicity of any kind. He also did not care about being cheated. He had no education. He would eat if there was something to eat, if not he was content to chew cud. If there was nothing to chew he would simply drink water and go to sleep. But when guests arrived he had to leave this path of contentment. Especially if they were sadhus—then he had to worry about worldly affairs. He could have gone to sleep with an empty stomach but could not leave the sadhu hungry. He was truly a devoted soul.

One day a mahatma came and parked himself on his doorstep. His face was majestic; he was wearing a *pitambar*, a yellow scarf, around his neck, had matted hair on his head, a brass kamandal in hand, wooden slippers on his feet and a pair of spectacles on his face. His whole demeanour was like that of the mahatmas who frequent the houses of nobles, make rounds of temples on aircrafts, and eat delicious food to achieve excellence in yoga. In these times such mahatmas find it difficult to digest coarse wheat. Shankar was anxious about how to feed the mahatma. Finally, he decided to borrow wheat from someone. He couldn't find wheat flour in the whole village. There were only ordinary people in the village, and no deities, so how would one find divine feed there? Fortunately, he found some wheat in the house of the village priest, a Brahmin. He borrowed one and a quarter ser of wheat grains and asked his wife to grind them. The mahatma ate that and slept soundly. When he got up in the morning he gave them his blessings and was on his way.

The Brahmin collected alms twice a year. Shankar thought, 'What's the point in returning one and a quarter ser of wheat? Instead, I will increase his alms. He'll understand, and I'll understand.' In the month of Chait, when the Brahmin arrived to collect his alms Shankar gave him nearly one and a quarter ser of wheat and thought himself free of his debt, and did not mention the matter. The Brahmin also did not ask for it a second time. How did the simple-minded Shankar know that he would have to take birth again to pay off the debt of one and a quarter ser of wheat?

2

Seven years passed. From a priest, the Brahmin became a moneylender, and from a peasant Shankar became a day labourer. Mangal, his younger brother, separated from him to live independently. When they lived together as a joint family, they were peasants. Separated, each one of them became a day labourer. Shankar hoped they would part without bitterness, but he was helpless in the face of the circumstances. The day food was cooked separately, he cried. The two brothers turned into enemies from that day. If one cried, the other would laugh; if there was mourning in one house, the other house would celebrate. The bond of love, of blood, and of milk was snapped. Shankar had built the family honour through hard work and maintained it through his life blood. But his heart now broke to pieces to see it besmirched. He refused to eat food for seven days. He worked right through the day in the scorching sun of Jaishta, and at night he covered his face and went to sleep. The hard work and unbearable pain ate into his vitals. He fell sick and remained bedridden for months. How would he run his family? He now had only half the portion of the five bighas of family land and one ox. How could he maintain himself as a peasant? Eventually, cultivation remained only a means of family honour. For livelihood he had to become a day labourer.

One day, when Shankar was returning from his day's work the Brahmin stopped him on the way and said, 'Shankar, come tomorrow to settle the accounts of your loan and interest. You have owed me five and a half maund of wheat for ages, and you show no sign of paying up! What are your intentions?'

Shankar was surprised. 'When did I borrow five and a half maund of wheat from you? You forget I don't owe anyone even a fistful of grains or a single paisa!'

'It's because of this nature of yours that you don't have enough to eat.' The Brahmin then reminded Shankar of the one and a quarter ser of wheat that he had lent him seven years ago. Shankar was stunned. *Oh God, how many times*

One and a Quarter *Ser* of Wheat

have I given him alms; what work of mine did he ever do? Whenever he came to my house to consult the almanac or tell the auspicious hour for some event, he always took some 'rewards'. What selfishness is this? One and a quarter ser of grains has now taken on this monstrous proportion—it will gobble me up! If he had given me an inkling I would've given him the appropriate measure of wheat as repayment. Was he silent all this while so he could make more out of me? He said, 'Maharaj, it is true I haven't given you grains of the exact measure saying that it was to pay off your debt, but several times I have given you alms to the measure of one ser or even two ser. Today you're asking for five and a half maund! Where can I get that from?'

The Brahmin asserted, 'Whatever is written in the ledger stands as it is, though the rewards may be hundred fold. Five and a half maund is written against your name in the ledger, you can send anyone to examine the accounts. You pay up and I'll strike off your name; if you don't, it will go on increasing.'

Shankar pleaded, 'Why are you tormenting a poor man like me? I cannot manage two square meals a day, where can I get so much wheat?'

'You can bring it from wherever you want. I'll not leave even a fistful of grains. If you don't pay now, you will have to pay in the hereafter.'

Shankar trembled in fear. *If the statement was made to an educated person like us, he would have said, 'It's all right, I'll pay in the hereafter. The measure there would not be greater than here. At least, why should I worry when there's no proof of the debt?'* But Shankar was neither clever nor argumentative. A debt from a Brahmin . . . if the name remained in the ledger, it meant he would directly go to hell. The mere thought made his hair stand on end. He said, 'Maharaj, I'll pay your debt here, why are you bringing God into it? I am being pushed around in this birth, why should I sow a thorn for the next one? But this is no justice. You have made a mountain out of a molehill. Being a Brahmin you should not have done that. If you had asked for it earlier I would have paid up, and this huge burden would not have fallen on me. I will pay up for sure, but you will have to answer before God.'

'You might be afraid of the hereafter, why should I be? I will have my brothers and friends there. The sages and seers are all Brahmin; God is also Brahmin, whatever the situation is, they will manage it. Now tell me, when are you paying up?'

'I do not have any in my house. I can pay you only if I borrow from someone.'

'That does not make me very happy. It has been seven years, now I cannot spare you even a day. If you cannot return the wheat, you have to sign a bond.'

'I know I have to pay up. You can take the wheat or you can make me sign a bond. What price will you put on the wheat?'

'The market rate is five sers; I'll draw the bond at the rate of five and a quarter ser.'

'If I have to pay, I'll do it at the market rate. Why should I be blamed for leaving the quarter?'

Sixty rupees was calculated to be the price of the wheat. A bond was drawn out for sixty rupees at a three per cent interest. If not paid within a year the rate of interest would be charged at three and a half per cent. Over and above that, Shankar had to pay eight annas for the stamp paper and one rupee for drawing the document.

The people of the entire village spoke ill of the Brahmin, but not to his face. Everyone needed the moneylender, so no one wanted to rub him the wrong way.

3

Shankar worked hard for one year. He had vowed to pay off the debt before the date was over. No cooking was done before afternoon. They used to live on gram, now they stopped that too. Rotis were made only for their son and that too at night. Shankar used to smoke tobacco worth one rupee earlier—it was his only addiction, which he could not do without. Now he had to sacrifice even that for the vow. He threw away the chillum, broke the hookah and smashed the tobacco bowl. He had already given up clothes to a great extent; now he only wore the barest minimum, to simply cover his nakedness. He spent the bone-chilling winter sitting near the fire. His firm resolve bore fruit beyond his expectation. At the end of the year he managed to collect sixty rupees. He had thought he would hand over the money to the Brahmin and say, 'Maharaj, I shall pay the balance as soon as possible.' It was just a matter of fifteen rupees. Panditji would surely agree to it. He took the money and gave it to the Brahmin who asked, surprised, 'Have you borrowed it from somebody?'

'No, Maharaj. With your blessings I got good wages.'

'But there are only sixty rupees!'

'Yes, Maharaj, take this now. The rest I'll pay in the next two or three months. Please release me.'

'You'll be released when you pay every paisa of mine. Go and bring me fifteen rupees.'

'Maharaj, show me some mercy. I do not have anything to eat in the evening. I live in this village; I'll pay you sometime in the future.'

'I do not appreciate these excuses, nor do I care for such glib talk. If you do not pay the entire amount, you will have to pay interest at the rate of three per cent from today. You can keep your money with you or leave it here.'

'All right. Please keep the amount I've brought you. I'll go and try to manage fifteen rupees from somewhere.'

Shankar tried everyone in the village but no one gave him money. This was not because they did not trust Shankar or they did not have money to lend. It was because no one had the courage to interfere with the Brahmin's prey.

4

Reaction after an action is a principle of nature. When Shankar could not free himself after the hard work of an entire year his hope turned into despair. He realized that even after undergoing so much hardship if he could not collect more than sixty rupees, he had no other means through which he could earn double the amount. If he had to carry the burden of debt on his head how did it matter whether the burden was big or small? His enthusiasm waned and he began to despise hard work. Hope begets enthusiasm, hope is strength, hope is life. It is hope that moves the world. Devoid of hope, Shankar became listless. The necessities of life that he had ignored the entire year could not be ignored any more. There was a limit to the patches he could stitch on his rags. Now if he got some money, he bought clothes or some foodstuff. He'd smoked tobacco earlier, now he added hemp and weeds to it. He was no longer worried about paying off the loan. He behaved as though he had no debt at all! Earlier, he'd go to work without fail even if he was sick. Now he looked for excuses to shirk work.

Three years passed in this way. The Brahmin did not ask him to pay up even once. Like an expert hunter he wanted to target his prey unawares. To forewarn the prey was against his principle.

One day Panditji called Shankar and showed him the accounts. After deducting the sixty rupees that Shankar had paid earlier, the balance now stood at one hundred and twenty.

'I can't pay this much money in this birth, I'll pay you in my next birth.'

'I'll take it right in this birth. If not the principal, you must pay the interest.'

'I have just one ox, take it. I have a hut, take it. What else do I have?'

'What shall I do with your ox or hut? You have a lot to give me.'

'What do I have, Maharaj?'

'If nothing, you at least have your own self. After all, you go to work for others for wages. I also have to employ labourers for my fields. You can work for me to pay the interest. Whenever it is convenient, you can pay the principal. Honestly, you cannot go to work to other places as long as you haven't paid my money. You have no property of your own. How can I leave such a huge debt without any security? Who can guarantee that you'll pay me interest every month? When you couldn't pay me the interest by working elsewhere, how can you pay the principal?'

'Maharaj, I'll work to pay the interest, but what shall I eat?'

'You have your wife and sons. Will they sit idle? As for me, I'll give you half a ser of maize every day, and you'll get one blanket per year. A *mirzai*, too. What else do you need? It's true that others give you six annas a day. But I do not require your full services. I am keeping you so that you can pay back the loan.'

Shankar thought deeply for some time. Then he said, 'That means bonded labour for life!'

'Call it slavery or labour, I'm not going to leave you as long as you haven't paid back the loan. If you run away, your son shall pay. Of course, it's a different matter when you are no more.'

There was no appeal against this decision. Who was there to bail him out? There was no refuge. Where would he run? He started working at the Brahmin's household from the next day. Just for one and a quarter ser of wheat he had to wear the fetters of slavery on his feet for life. If the poor fellow could derive some consolation it was from the thought that it was the consequence of his deeds in his previous birth. His wife had to do the kind of jobs she had not done earlier. The children had to beg for every morsel. Shankar could do nothing except watch all this helplessly. Like a curse from a God he couldn't shake off the burden of the wheat grains from his head for the rest of his life.

5

Shankar worked as a bonded labourer for the Brahmin for twenty years before he died. He still had a debt of one hundred and twenty rupees against his name. Panditji did not consider it proper to blame him in the court of God. He was not that unjust or cruel. He grabbed Shankar's young son. He still works in his house. No one knows when he will be released, or whether he will be released at all. Only God knows.

Dear reader, do not think that this narrative is an imaginary one. It is true. The world is not devoid of such Shankars and such Brahmins.

Translated from the Hindi by M. Asaduddin

The Woman Who Sold Grass

1

Mulia came in with bundles of freshly cut grass, her wheatish complexion flushed and her large intoxicating eyes filled with apprehension. Seeing her, Mahaveer asked, 'What happened, Mulia, how are you feeling today?'

Mulia didn't answer, her eyes were teary.

Mahaveer came closer and asked, 'What happened, why don't you tell me? Has someone said something? Has mother scolded you? Why are you sad?'

Mulia said, sobbing, 'Nothing. What could have happened? I'm fine.'

Mahaveer looked at Mulia from head to toe, 'Are you going to cry in secret? Won't you tell me?'

Dodging the question, Mulia said, 'There's got to be something to tell, what should I say?'

Mulia was a rose in that desert. She had a wheatish complexion, doe-like eyes, an elongated chin, slightly rosy cheeks, long pointed eyelashes and unusually sparkling eyes that clearly reflected a pain, a mute anguish. Who knows how this angel had descended into that home of Chamars! Was her soft, flower-like body made to carry a basket of grass on the head for selling? There were people in the village willing to dance to her tunes, who yearned for a glance from her, who would feel uplifted by even a single word from her but she had been there longer than a year and no one had seen her glance at or talk to these youths. When she stepped out with her grass, it felt as if the light of dawn, dressed in gold, was going past, evenly scattering its rays. Seeing her, some serenaded her, others put their hands to their hearts but Mulia went by silently with her eyes lowered. People would exclaim with amazement, 'Such pride! And what is special about Mahaveer anyway? He is not in the prime of his life; God knows how she lives with him!'

But that day something had happened which other women of this community might keep secret, but for Mulia it was like a stake through her heart. That morning the fragrance of mango blossoms danced in the breeze, the sky seemed to shower gold on the earth. When, with the basket on her head, Mulia stepped out to cut grass, the rays of the morning sun transformed her dusky colour into gold. Suddenly, Chain Singh appeared before her. Mulia wanted to slink away but Chain Singh grabbed her hand and said, 'Mulia, don't you feel any pity for me at all?'

Mulia's flower-like face ignited like a volcano. She wasn't the least bit afraid and didn't hesitate for a moment; she put down her basket and said, 'Leave me or I'll shout.' Chain Singh experienced something new that day. What use was beauty and grace in lower-caste women if not to be playthings for the upper castes? He had achieved many such feats but Mulia's countenance, her anger and pride, shocked him out of his wits. Embarrassed, he let go of her hand. Mulia strode ahead. In the heat of the battle you don't feel the pain; it's only later that it hurts. Having walked some distance, Mulia realized how angry and afraid she was, how helpless, and her eyes filled with tears. She tried to hold them back but soon she was sobbing. If she hadn't been so poor, who would have dared to insult her! She kept crying as she cut the grass. She knew Mahaveer's temper. If she told him, he'd be out for the Thakur's blood, and who knows what would happen then! She got goosebumps at the very thought of it. That's why she didn't answer Mahaveer's questions.

2

The next day Mulia did not go to cut grass. Her mother-in-law asked, 'Why don't you go? All the others have gone.'

Mulia lowered her head and said, 'I won't go alone.'

'Do you think you'll be carried off by a tiger?' her mother-in-law said in a rage.

Mulia bent her head even further and said in a low voice, 'Everybody teases me.'

The mother-in-law chided her, 'You don't want to go with the others and you don't want to go alone. Why don't you say clearly that you don't want to go at all? You can't carry on like a queen in my house. No one cares much for your beauty, they want their work done. You are very beautiful but can I live on your beauty? Take the basket and go get grass.'

Mahaveer was rubbing down the horse under the shadow of the neem tree by the door. He saw Mulia leaving with a tearful face but he couldn't say anything. If he had his way, he would keep her close to his heart and before his eyes, but the horse needed to be fed. If he bought grass, it would cost him no less than twelve annas a day. He sometimes managed to earn a rupee or two but there was no guarantee. And where could he earn that kind of money? He hardly earned one and a half or two rupees; he was able to sometimes and sometimes he was not. Ever since these ruinous lorries had been introduced, the *ekkawalas*' animals had gone out of work. Nobody even wants to travel for free. He'd bought the ekka and the horse with a loan of a hundred and fifty rupees from the moneylender, but who cares for ekkas when there are lorries? He couldn't pay back the moneylender—not even the interest, forget the principal!

He said half-heartedly, 'If you don't feel like going, let it be, we'll see.'

This show of sympathy pleased Mulia. 'What will the horse eat?' she asked.

She avoided yesterday's path today and walked between the mounds on the fields. She kept looking around cautiously. Sugar-cane fields lay on both sides. Even the smallest sound numbed her—what if someone was hiding in the sugar cane? But nothing happened. She passed the sugar-cane fields and the mango orchards; irrigated lands came into view. A pulley was running in a well in the distance. The mounds of earth in the fields were thick with green grass. Greed came over Mulia. In half an hour she could gather more grass here than what a dry field would yield over the entire afternoon! Nobody keeps watch over here. If somebody shouts, I'll leave. She squatted and started skinning the grass, and in an hour's time more than half her basket was full. She was so engrossed in her work that she didn't notice Chain Singh coming. When she suddenly raised her head at the sound of footsteps, she saw him before her.

Mulia's heart froze. She wanted to run, to turn over the basket and go home with the empty basket but Chain Singh said from some yards away, 'Don't be afraid, don't be afraid, for God's sake! I won't trouble you. Take as much grass as you want, it's my field.'

Mulia's hands were numb, the small hoe remained glued to her hand and she couldn't even see the grass. She wanted the ground to open and swallow her. The world seemed to float in front of her eyes.

Chain Singh asked reassuringly, 'Why don't you cut? Have I ever made an objection? Come out here every day, I'll help you cut too.'

Mulia was as still as a painted figure.

Chain Singh took a step forward and said, 'Why are you so scared of me! You think I've come to trouble you again? God knows that yesterday too I didn't take your hand to harass you. Seeing you, my hand just moved on its own. I lost my mind. You went away; I sat there crying for hours. I felt like chopping off my hand. I felt like consuming poison. I've been searching for you since and finally you came this way. Looking for you everywhere, I ended up here. You can punish me as much as you want. Even if you decide to chop my head off, my neck won't tremble. I was a rogue, a loafer, but after seeing you, I've been cleansed of all wickedness. I wish I were your dog and could follow you everywhere, or your horse whom you feed grass with your hands. If only this follower of yours could be of some use to you. My youth is cursed if I say this insincerely! Mahaveer is lucky to have got an angel like you.'

Mulia had been listening quietly and now, lowering her head, asked innocently, 'So what do you want me to do?'

Chain Singh came closer and said, 'I want only your kindness.'

Mulia looked up and glanced at him. Her sense of shame had vanished. She said sharply, 'Can I ask you something? Don't mind. Are you married?'

Chain Singh replied in a suppressed voice, 'Yes I am married, but what is marriage, it's only a game.'

A scornful smile played on Mulia's lips. She said, 'Still, if my man spoke to your woman like this, how would you feel? Wouldn't you be ready to chop his head off? Speak! What do you think—that Mahaveer is a Chamar so there's no blood in his veins, he has no sense of shame, no idea about his dignity. You are fond of my looks. Don't women many times more beautiful wander near the ghats? I can't even be compared to the soles of their feet. Why don't you appeal to one of them? Are they lacking in pity? But you won't go there because it wounds your heart to do that. You dare to ask me because I'm a chamarin, from the lower caste, and women from the lower caste, with a little threatening and tempting, can be easily caught in your fist. It's a cheap bargain. You're a Thakur, why would you let such a chance pass?'

Embarrassed, Chain Singh said, 'Mulia, that's not true. I'm telling you the truth. It's not a matter of high or low birth. Everybody is equal. I'm willing to place my head at your feet.'

Mulia said, 'That's because you know I can't do a thing. Go place your head at the feet of a Kshatriya woman and then you'll see the outcome of placing your head at the feet of a woman. Your head won't be left standing on your neck.'

Chain Singh was sinking into the ground in shame. His face had the withered look of someone who has just spent months on the sickbed. No words came out of his mouth. Mulia was outspoken without being proud.

She spoke again, 'I go to the market every day, I know what goes on in the big houses. Is there one well-to-do home which doesn't employ a syce, a coachman, a water-carrier, a priest and a cook? All these people are diversions for the rich. Whatever those rich women do, they're right in doing! Don't their husbands go around losing their hearts to *chamarin*s and *kaharin*s? The give and take is even. But the poor have no such means. I am everything to my husband. He would never even glance at another woman. It's a matter of chance that I'm a little pretty but even if I were black and ugly, he would treat me the same. I'm quite sure about it. I may be a chamarin but I will not stoop so low as to repay his faith with deception. Yes, if he starts following his fancies, if he makes me suffer, then I'll do the same to him. You're crazy about my looks, aren't you? If I suddenly grow pockmarked, if I turn blind in one eye, you won't even spare me a glance. Tell me, am I lying?'

Chain Singh could not deny it.

Mulia continued in the same proud tone, 'If I turn blind in not just one but both eyes, he will still treat me the same way. He will nurse me and feed me. You want me to cheat such a person? Go! And never tease me again, or it won't be good for you.'

3

Youth is passion, strength, kindness, courage, self-confidence, honour and everything that makes life sacred, bright and complete. Youth is intoxicated with pride, cruelty, selfishness, impertinence, material love, wickedness and all that leads life towards beastliness, deterioration and ruin. Chain Singh was drunk on youth. Mulia's cool nature brought him back to his senses just as a splash of water poured over boiling syrup rids it of its impurities and a clear, pure liquid comes forth. Chain Singh's youthful obsession had been sent packing, only youth remained. The words of a beautiful woman can as easily make one lose one's faith as they can bring deliverance.

Chain Singh was a changed man from that day on. He had been short-tempered, used to swearing at, scolding and beating up his workmen over small things. The powerless trembled before him. The labourers would get busy with their work whenever they saw him approaching but no sooner had he turned his back than they'd start smoking their chillums. In their hearts, everybody hated him and bad-mouthed him. But from that day on, Chain Singh became so kind-hearted, so serious and patient that the people were awestruck.

Many days passed. One evening Chain Singh went on an inspection of his farm. Water was being drawn there for irrigation. He saw that the canal had cracked in one place and water was running waste. It wasn't reaching the beds but the old woman who had made them was sitting idly by. She didn't seem concerned about finding out why the water wasn't reaching the beds. If he'd seen this happen earlier, Chain Singh would have lost it. He would have cut the woman's wages for the day, and snarled at the workers operating the pulley, but that day he stayed calm. He took some clay and bound the fissure on the canal; then he went into the field and said to the old woman, 'You're sitting here while all the water is running waste.'

Agitated, the old woman said, 'It must have opened just now, my master! I'll go right now and fix it.'

She was trembling as she said this. Calming her, Chain Singh said, 'Don't run away, don't run away, I've closed the canal. Haven't seen the old man for many days. Does he go to work or not?'

Delighted, the old woman said, 'He's sitting idle nowadays, Bhaiya, there's nowhere for him to work.'

Chain Singh said gently, 'So put him to work with me. There's a little hemp, tell him to cut it.'

Having said this, he went towards the well. Four pulleys were at work there but two of the four labourers had gone off to eat *ber*. The other two were stunned to see Chain Singh. If the Thakur asks about the others, what will we say? All of us will be scolded. Poor creatures, they were squirming inside. Chain Singh asked, 'Where have those two gone?'

No sound came from either of their mouths. Suddenly, the other two could be seen making their way; each had bers tucked into a corner of his dhoti. They were chatting gaily as they walked but as soon as they saw Chain Singh, they shrivelled up with fear. Each foot felt as heavy as a quintal. They could neither move forward nor go back. Both knew that they'd be scolded and that their wages might be withheld as well; this slowed them down. Chain Singh called out to them, 'Come on, come on, what are the bers like, let me sample them, they're from my tree, aren't they?'

The two men were even more terrified. The Thakur won't leave us alive today. See how sweetly he speaks. That's exactly how brutally he'll beat us. The poor things were withering away. Chain Singh said again, 'Get here at once, I'll take all the ripe ones. One of you run home and get some salt. (To the other two workers) You two also join us; the bers from that tree are sweet. Eat some bers; work will always go on.'

Now the two truants were a little encouraged. They put all the bers before Chain Singh and started picking out the ripe ones for him. One of them ran to fetch some salt. For half an hour the pulleys stayed still. When all the bers were eaten and Chain Singh made to leave, the two offenders joined their hands. 'Bhaiyaji, please spare us today, we were very hungry or we wouldn't have gone.'

Chain Singh said softly, 'So, what's wrong with that? I had ber too. And we wasted an hour or so, that's all. If you want, you can do an hour's work in half an hour. If you don't want to do it, then even an hour's work can't be finished over a whole day.'

Chain Singh left, and the four of them fell into a discussion.

First: 'If the master stays like this, one would feel like working. It's difficult to work when someone's always breathing down your neck.'

Second: 'I thought he would eat us alive today.'

Third: 'I've been noticing him for some days, he's grown softer.'

Fourth: 'Let's see if we get a full day's wages in the evening, then we'll talk.'

First: 'You're so dim-witted. You can't even judge a person's countenance.'

Second: 'We should work whole-heartedly now.'

Third: 'Of course! When he has shown faith in us, it's our duty to do our best.'

Fourth: 'As for me, folks, I still can't trust the Thakur.'

4

Chain Singh had to go to court on work one day. It was a journey of about five miles. He usually went on horseback but the sun was quite harsh that day, so he decided to take an ekka instead. Mahaveer was sent word that he should take him along. Mahaveer called out to him at about nine o'clock. Chain Singh was ready; he quickly mounted the ekka. But the horse was so emaciated, the seat so dirty and tattered, everything so shabby, that Chain Singh was embarrassed to sit on it. He asked, 'Why is all this stuff in such a bad condition, Mahaveer? Your horse was never so feeble. Are there very few passengers these days?' Mahaveer said, 'No, master, there are passengers, but who asks for an ekka when there are lorries? I'd go home with two or three rupees earlier, I now hardly even get twenty annas. What should I feed the horse and what should I eat myself? I'm in big trouble. I'm thinking of selling off the ekka and the horse and working for those like you, but it's hard to find takers. A sum of at least twelve annas goes on the horse, not counting the grass. When we go hungry most of the time, who is going to care for the horse?'

Chain Singh looked at his torn kurta and said, 'Why don't you farm some two or three bighas of land?'

Mahaveer bowed his head and said, 'Farming takes a lot of hard work. I'm thinking that if I get a client, I'll remove the ekka's spare parts and use it for ferrying grass to the market. Both my mother and wife go out to gather grass these days. That's the only way ten or twelve annas come my way.'

Chain Singh asked, 'So the old woman goes to the market?'

Mahaveer said shamefaced, 'No, Bhaiya, how could she walk so far? My wife goes. She cuts grass till the afternoon and then heads to the market. By the time she returns, it's late at night. It's hard, but what to do, how does one fight one's fate?'

Chain Singh reached the court and Mahaveer, taking his ekka this way and that in search of passengers, went into the city. Chain Singh asked him to return by five.

At about four, Chain Singh emerged from his work. There was a paan shop nearby and a little further on a large banyan tree in whose shade stood dozens of tongas, ekkas and phaetons. The horses had been untied. These were the carriages of lawyers, attorneys and officers. Chain Singh drank some water, had a paan and thought that if he got a lorry he would head to town for a bit, when his eye fell on a grass-cutter woman. With a basketful of grass on her head, she was bargaining with the syces. Chain Singh's heart leapt with joy—it was Mulia! She was dressed up nicely in a pink sari and was bargaining with the coachmen. Many coachmen had gathered; some bantered with her, some stared, some laughed at her.

A coal-dark coachman said to her, 'Mula, the grass is, at the very most, worth six annas.'

Mulia stared at him with her passion-arousing eyes and said, 'If you want it in six annas, the grass-cutters are sitting over there. Go on, you'll get it for two to four paisa less. But my grass you won't get for less than twelve annas.'

A middle-aged coachman said from atop his phaeton, 'It's your day, why twelve annas, ask for a rupee. The takers will take it boastfully. The lawyers are about to come out, there isn't much time left.'

A tongawala in a pink turban said, 'The old man's mouth is watering, why would Mulia spare us a glance now?'

Chain Singh was so furious he wanted to hit these scoundrels with his shoes. How everyone is staring at her, as if they will drink her up with their eyes. And Mulia is so happy here. She isn't shying away or hesitating or submitting. How, passing around smiles, looking about with her attractive eyes, sliding her sari further and further off her head, turning her face at everyone, she speaks. The same Mulia who had roared like a lioness at him!

It was now four o'clock. A carnival of agents, lawyers and attorneys appeared. The agents ran towards the lorries. The lawyers and attorneys headed to their carriages. The coachmen quickly readied their horses. Many of the dignitaries ogled lustily at Mulia as they boarded their vehicles.

Suddenly Mulia took her basket and ran after a phaeton. A young lawyer sahib turned out in the English fashion sat in it. He got Mulia to keep the grass on the footstep and, taking out something from his pocket, handed it to her. Mulia smiled, the two said something to each other, which Chain Singh could not hear.

In the next instant, Mulia, happy-faced, was heading home. Chain Singh, hypnotized, remained standing near the paan shop. When the shopkeeper wound up, put on his clothes, shut the door of his cabin and came down, Chain Singh came to life. He asked, 'Have you closed your shop?'

The shopkeeper said sympathetically, 'Please get some treatment for this, Thakur Sahib, this illness is not a good thing!'

Chain Singh was astonished and asked, 'What illness?'

The shopkeeper said, 'What illness! You've been standing here for the last half an hour as if you were dead. The court has emptied, all the shops have closed, even the sweepers have gone—have you noticed anything? This is a serious illness, get it treated quickly.'

Chain Singh took his stick and went to the gate and saw Mahaveer's ekka coming towards him.

5

When some distance had been covered, Chain Singh asked, 'How much did you earn today, Mahaveer?'

Mahaveer laughed and said, 'Master, today I was left waiting all day. Nobody wanted a ride even for free. On top of that I smoked bidis for four paise.'

After a while Chain Singh said, 'I have some advice for you. You take a rupee from me every day, and whenever I call for you come over with your ekka. Then your wife won't have to go with grass to the market. Do you agree?'

Mahaveer looked at him with bright eyes and said, 'Master, I eat your salt, I am your subject. Whenever you want, just call for me. To take money from you—'

Chain Singh interrupted, 'No, I don't want free service from you. Come and get a rupee from me every day. Don't send your wife with grass to the market. Your honour is my honour. And whenever you need more money, don't hesitate to come and get it. Yes, and see to it that you don't discuss this matter with Mulia. What's the use!'

One evening, many days later, Mulia happened to meet Chain Singh. Having finished his transactions with his debtors, he was heading home when, at the very spot where he had seized Mulia's hand, her voice came to him. Chain Singh stopped short and looked back to see Mulia running towards him. He said, 'What is it, Mula? Why do you run when I am waiting for you?'

Mulia was panting and said, 'I've wanted to meet you for many days. When I saw you coming, I ran. I don't go to sell grass these days.'

Chain Singh said, 'That's good.'

'Have you ever seen me selling grass?'

'Yes, I saw you one day. Has Mahaveer told you everything? I asked him not to.'

'He never hides anything from me.'

They stood quietly for a second. Neither knew what to say. Suddenly, Mulia said with a smile, 'This is where you held my hand.'

Chain Singh said in embarrassment, 'Forget about that, Mula. God knows what devil had possessed me.'

Mulia said in a faltering voice, 'Why should I forget about it? You're still fulfilling the obligation you took on by seizing my arm. Poverty makes people do what it will. You have saved me.'

They both fell silent again. After a little while Mulia said, 'You must have thought that I was oblivious to all that laughter and talk?'

Chain Singh said forcefully, 'No, Mulia, I didn't think that for even a moment.'

Mulia said with a smile, 'This is what I expected from you. And still expect.'

The air was coming down to rest on the furrowed fields, the sun was slipping away silently into the lap of the night, and in that dim light Chain Singh stood watching Mulia's figure slowly fade into the darkness.

*Translated from the Hindi by
Ranjeeta Dutta and Anjum Hasan*

The Mantra

1

There was magic in Pandit Leeladhar Choubey's words. Whenever he stood on a podium and showered the nectar of his voice on the audience, the souls of all those who listened were satiated and charmed, almost as if they had been intoxicated. Choubeyji's speeches carried little substance and even the wordplay was not very beautiful. Its effect, however, was not dulled even by repetition. On the contrary, it became more effective upon repetition, like the blows of a hammer. I do not believe this, but those who listen to him claim that he has memorized just one speech and repeats it verbatim in every assembly, though in a different style. Praising the Hindu community was the prime characteristic of his speeches. The moment he ascended a podium, he charmed everybody by his encomiums to the glory of ancient India and to the immortal fame of the ancestors. For instance:

> 'Good people! Whose eyes will not overflow with tears after listening to the tale of our utter degradation? When

we remember our ancient glory, it becomes doubtful if we are the same people or we have changed. One who could formerly challenge a lion to a duel now searches for a rat hole when he sees a mouse. There must be a limit to this decline. Why look far off when we can talk about Emperor Chandragupta's reign? A famous Greek historian records that in that age, doors were never locked here, thefts were unheard of, there was no promiscuity, documents had not been invented, lakhs were exchanged on mere chits, and judges passed their time swatting flies! Good people! In those days, no man died young. (Applause) I repeat, in those days, no man died young. A son passing away before his father was an unprecedented—in fact, impossible—event. In this age, how many such parents can be found whose hearts have not been blighted by the demise of a youthful son? It is not the same India any more. India has come undone.'

Such was Choubeyji's style. He kindled people's nationalistic pride by lamenting the present fallen and pitiable condition, and singing paeans to the prosperity and glory of the past. It was for this accomplishment that he was counted as one among the leaders. In particular, he was considered the flag-bearer of the Hindu Sabha. Among the Sabha's followers, there was none as enthusiastic, as competent or as diplomatic. It can be said that he had devoted his life to the Sabha's cause. Surely, he was not wealthy. At least this is what people believed, but he did have the invaluable gems of courage, patience and wisdom, and all this had been dedicated to the Sabha. In fact, he was the life of the *shuddhi* movement. He believed that the rise and fall, and the life and death of Hindu society was predicated on this very question. There could not be a way other than shuddhi for the resurgence of Hindus. The panacea for the moral, physical, psychological, social, economic and religious ills of the community was dependent on the success of this very movement, and his body and mind were both industriously engaged in it. He was especially competent at collecting donations. God had granted him that special knowledge by which even stones could be turned pliable. His dealings with misers were like the strokes of a blunt knife—the gentlemen learnt a lesson they'd never forget! In this matter, he employed all kinds of persuasion, enticement, punishment and deceit. So much so that he even considered robbery and theft to be forgivable, if undertaken in the interest of the nation.

2

It was the summer season and Panditji was making preparations for a sojourn in a cool, hilly region. It would be an outing, and if the opportunity arose, he could collect some donations too. Whenever he desired a tour, he would set out with a group of friends as a deputation. Who loses anything if out of a collection of one thousand rupees, half was spent on his tours? By this arrangement, the Hindu Sabha also received some money. None would be collected but for his efforts! This time around, Panditji decided to take his family along. His financial condition, which was hitherto a cause for concern, had become quite stable since the emergence of the shuddhi movement.

How can the devotees of community welfare have the good fortune of experiencing the pleasure of living in peace? In fact, they were born to wander around aimlessly. There was word about the *Tablighi*s wreaking havoc in the Madras province. Village after village of Hindus was embracing Islam. The maulvis were promoting the Tablighi movement with great fervour. If the Hindu Sabha did nothing to stop this current, the entire province would be emptied of Hindus. It would be impossible to spot a single Hindu!

All hell broke loose in the Hindu Sabha. Immediately, a special session was convened and the problem was presented before the leaders. After much deliberation, it was decided that Choubeyji must be entrusted with this responsibility. He must be requested to proceed to Madras at once and rescue the converted brothers.

It only needed to be said once. Choubeyji, who had anyway dedicated himself to the service of the Hindu community, gave up the idea of a mountain tour and agreed to visit Madras. With tears in his eyes, the Hindu Sabha minister requested him, 'Sir, you alone can shoulder this responsibility. God has granted these powers to you alone. There is no man in this great India, except you, who can be of help during such a calamity. Have pity on the fallen condition of the community.' Choubeyji could not decline this prayer. A group of volunteers was promptly constituted and it set out under Panditji's leadership. A grand farewell feast was given in his honour, a charitable rich man presented him with a purse, and thousands gathered at the railway station to bid him farewell.

Writing an account of the journey is not required. At every major station on the way, the volunteers were welcomed with honour. At many places, purses were presented. The Ratlam principality gifted an awning. A motor car was given by the Baroda principality so that volunteers would not have to suffer walking on foot. By the time they reached Madras, the volunteers' group had collected many other useful things, apart from a substantial sum.

In Madras, the Hindu Sabha camped in an open ground far from habitation. The national flag was raised above the camp. The volunteers put on their uniforms, local wealthy tycoons sent provisions for a feast and tents were pitched. The hustle-bustle was such that it seemed as if a king were camping there.

3

It was eight o'clock at night. Close to a settlement of untouchables, the camp of the volunteers was glittering under the gaslights. Many thousands had gathered, amongst whom most were untouchables. Separate burlap seating was laid out for them. The Hindus of higher castes were seated on carpets. Pandit Leeladhar's invigorating lecture was on. 'You are the children of the same seers who could create a new world beneath the heavens! The very same to whose justice, wisdom and intellect the entire world bows today.' Suddenly, an old untouchable man rose and questioned, 'Are we too children of the same seers?'

Leeladhar replied, 'Without doubt! The blood coursing through your veins is of the very same seers, and even though the cruel, hard-hearted, thoughtless and narrow-minded Hindu society of today looks down upon you with disdain, you are not inferior to any Hindu, no matter how superior he might consider himself to be.'

The old man countered, 'Then why does your Sabha not remember us in its programmes?'

Leeladhar said, 'The Hindu Sabha was founded just sometime ago, and they can be proud of whatever they have achieved in this short period. The Hindu community has woken up after centuries of slumber, and the time is nigh when, in India, no Hindu will think of another Hindu as inferior, and all will think of all as brothers. Lord Rama had embraced Nishada, who was a tribal, and accepted the half-eaten berries of Shabari, an untouchable—'

The old man countered again, 'If you are really the children of such great beings, why do you so wholly believe in the separation of the high and the low?'

Leeladhar tried to explain, 'Because we have fallen. Ignorance has made us forget those great souls.'

The old man continued, 'So now that your slumber is broken, will you eat with us?'

Leeladhar responded, 'I have no objection.'

The old man was not done yet, and threw another challenge, 'Will you have your daughter marry my son?'

Leeladhar, trying to save his face, said, 'Until you change your birth rituals, until your lifestyle has undergone a transformation, we cannot establish marital relations with you. Give up meat eating, give up alcohol drinking, accept education. Only then can you mingle with high-caste Hindus.'

Finally the old man burst out, 'We know many such high-born Brahmins who stay inebriated day and night, and do not eat a morsel without meat, and there are many who are also completely illiterate, but I see you dining with them. You will never refuse to have marital relations with them. When you yourself are wallowing in ignorance, how can you uplift us? Even now your heart is full of pride. Go and reform your soul for a few more days. You cannot uplift us even if you try. So long as we are part of the Hindu community, our foreheads will remain stained with the mark of inferiority. However learned we become, however genteel we become, you will think of us as inferior as you do now. The conscience of Hindus has died and arrogance has taken its place! Now we are taking refuge in that god whose followers are ready to embrace us as we are today. They do not demand that we join them by giving up our culture. Whether we are good or evil—they are calling out to us in our present condition. If you are high-born, stay high. We have no need of flying high.'

Leeladhar made a feeble attempt, 'Such words from a child of the seers astonish me. It was the seers who separated the varnas. How can you erase that?'

The old man fired the last salvo, 'Don't heap ignominy on the seers. All this false ritualism was invented by you people. You accuse us of drinking alcohol but you prostrate yourself before drunkards. You cringe from us because we eat meat, but you supplicate yourself before beef eaters. Only because they are more powerful than you! Today if we were to become kings, you would stand before us with folded hands. In your religion, the powerful are superior, and the powerless inferior. Is this your religion?'

Having said this, the old man left the gathering and many other people followed him. Only Choubeyji and some members of his group were left on the stage, like a recital's echo hanging in the air long after the performance has concluded.

4

When the Tablighis heard of Choubeyji's arrival, they were worried, anxious and determined to keep him away from the people. Choubeyji's name was known far and wide. The Tablighis knew that if he persisted there, all their own efforts would become futile. *He should not be allowed to plant his feet there.* The maulvis started thinking of a solution. After much debate, fuss and argument, it was decided that this kafir had to be assassinated. There was no shortage of men eager to earn such merit. The gates of paradise would open for such a man, the virgins of paradise would bless him, the angels would collect the dust of his feet as kohl, the Prophet will bless him with prosperity, and the godly would embrace him, calling him their dear friend. Two strong young men promptly assumed the responsibility.

It was past ten o'clock in the night. Silence spread across the Hindu Sabha camp. Only Choubeyji was awake in his tent, writing a letter to the minister of the Hindu Sabha. 'The greatest requirement here is that of money. Money! Money! Money! Send as much as you can. Send out deputations for collections, dig into the pockets of rich moneylenders, or beg. The unfortunate here cannot be uplifted without money. Unless a school is opened, a hospital is established, or there is a library, how will they believe that the Hindu Sabha is concerned about their welfare? If I can manage even half of what the Tablighis are spending, the standard of Hindu religion will fly high. Just speeches will not do the trick. Only blessings are not enough for survival.'

Suddenly he heard someone's footsteps and was startled. Raising his eyes, he saw two men standing there. Suspicious of them, Panditji inquired, 'Who are you? Why have you come here?' The response came, 'We are angels of Israel. We have come to capture your soul. Israel has summoned you.'

Panditji, who was otherwise a very strong man, could have pushed them to the ground with just one shove. In the morning, his breakfast comprised three quarters of semolina pudding and two litres of milk. For lunch he laced his dal with a quarter measure of ghee, and in the evening, he consumed hemp with milk, mixed with a ser of cream and half a ser of almonds. Then he ate a heavy dinner because after that he would not eat anything till morning. The crowning glory was that he never walked even one step! What pleasure if a palanquin could be arranged! It would feel as if his bed was flying through the air. If nothing, at least the buggy was there, although there were very few buggy drivers in Kashi who, when they saw Choubeyji, did not declare, 'The buggy is already hired.' In a wrestling mud pit, such a man could tire out an opponent just by lying flat on the ground and not moving at all. On occasions that required agility and swiftness, he proved to be a turtle out for a walk in the sand.

Panditji spied the door from the corner of his eye. There was no opportunity to escape. This infused some courage into him, courage which comes when the threshold of fear is breached. He reached for his cane and thundered, 'Get out of here!'

An attack of canes began even before he could complete his words. Panditji fell down unconscious. His enemies approached him for inspection and, finding no sign of life, took the mission to be accomplished. They had not planned to loot the place but what harm was there in reaching out for things when there was no one to question it? Whatever they could find, they gathered, and set off.

5

In the morning, when the old untouchable man strolled past the camp, there was absolute silence there. Not a soul could be seen! Even the tents had vanished! He wondered what the matter was. Everything had disappeared overnight, just like Aladdin's castles. Not even one of those who'd feasted on semolina pudding in the morning and churned hemp in the evening could be seen. As he went closer and peeped into Pandit Leeladhar's tent, his heart seemed to stop beating! Like a corpse, Panditji was lying on the ground. Flies buzzed around his mouth and blood had clotted in his hair like the colours of a painter's brush. His clothes too were soaked with blood. He understood that Panditji's companions had killed him and gone their own way. Suddenly, a cry of agony escaped Panditji mouth. The old man thought, 'There is still some life left.' The old man ran back to his village and gathered some men to carry Panditji to his own house.

Then began the dressing and nursing. The old man sat next to Panditji all day and night. His family members too busied themselves with serving Panditji and the villagers extended help in whatever capacity they could. They would argue, 'Which dear one of his is here? Familiar or stranger, we are the only ones. He came here to uplift us, otherwise what reason did he have to come here?' Panditji had taken ill many times at home too, but his family had not nursed him with such dedication. The whole family of the old man . . . in fact the whole village had devoted itself to Panditji's service. Selfishness that comes with civilization had not yet strangled the feeling of serving guests as if it was a religious duty. Even today the rustic shaman hurries and covers five or ten miles on foot to cure snakebites, even on a dark, overcast winter night. He does not double his fee or demand a ride. The old man even cleaned Panditji's natural waste, ignored his reprimands, and begged the entire village for milk for Panditji. And he did all this without ever complaining about it. If his family neglected Panditji while he was away, he would scold everybody when he returned.

Panditji recuperated after a month and it was only then that he came to know the extent of their beneficence. He realized, 'It was these people's efforts that saved me from the jaws of death, otherwise was I not already dead? The people whom I considered lowly and whose uplift I took up as my responsibility are far greater than me. In a situation like this I would have just sent the patient to a hospital and prided myself on my dutifulness, and would have believed that I had brought glory to ancestors like Dadhichi and Harishchandra.' Every hair on his body blessed these godlike people.

6

Three months passed in this manner. Neither the Hindu Sabha nor Panditji's family sought any news of him. The Sabha mouthpiece shed tears on his death and praised his work. A fund was instituted to collect money for building a memorial to him. His own family gave up the matter after some mourning.

Far away, Panditji was fortifying his body on a diet of milk and ghee. His face was flushed with a greatly rejuvenated blood flow and his body too became healthy. The country climate achieved what at one time could not be achieved by cream and butter. Although he was now not as presentable as before, he did become doubly swift and agile. There was no trace of the earlier sloth that was caused by obesity. New life was infused into him.

Winter had begun. Panditji was making preparations for returning home. Meanwhile, the village was struck by plague and three men fell sick. The old Chaudhuri was among them. Their families fled, abandoning them. Abandoning patients suffering from diseases, considered to be a curse of the goddess, was a custom in that village. Saving them was tantamount to confronting the gods, and where could they flee after such confrontation? How could they dare to snatch away God's chosen ones? They tried to take Panditji along with them but he refused. He decided to stay put in the village and try and save the sick. In such a situation, how could he abandon the man who had pulled him out of the jaws of death? Beneficence had awakened his soul. On the third day, when the old man regained consciousness and found Panditji standing next to him, he said, 'Sir, why have you come here?

The gods have summoned me to them. There is no way I can live any more. Why should you put your own life in danger? Have mercy on me. Leave.'

This had no effect on Panditji. He would go to the three patients by turns and treat their tonsils or tell them stories from the Puranas. There were provisions, utensils and other such things lying about in the houses abandoned by their owners. Panditji used these to concoct potions and feed them. At night, when the patients slept and the entire village felt eerie and haunted, Panditji had visions of ferocious beings. Out of fear, his heartbeat would rise, but his resolve to stay back was not weakened. He had decided that either he would save these men or sacrifice himself for them. When the patients' condition did not improve even after three days of nursing, Panditji was greatly worried. The town was ten miles away. There were no railways around, the road passed through the wilderness and there was no other transport available. Panditji was also concerned about what might happen to the patients if they were left alone. A hapless Panditji was greatly troubled. Finally, on the fourth day, when dawn was still a quarter of the night away, he left for the city on foot and reached there at about ten in the morning. He had to face great difficulty in obtaining medicines from the hospital, where the authorities were charging obnoxious rates from the rustic villagers for the medicines. Why would they give it to Panditji for free? Addressing his assistant though it was intended for Panditji, the doctor said, 'The medicine is not ready.'

Panditji pleaded, 'Sir, I have come from very far. Many people are lying sick. Without the medicine, all of them will perish.'

The assistant replied with irritation, 'Why are you bothering me? I've told you the medicine is not ready, nor can it be prepared in such a hurry.'

Panditji pleaded again, abasing himself, 'Sir, I am a Brahmin. May God make your children live long. Have mercy. May your glory last long.'

How can a corrupt worker have the quality of mercy? They are vassals to money. The more Panditji pleaded with him, the more annoyed he became. Never in his life had Panditji demeaned himself in this manner. At that moment, he did not have even a dime with him. If he had known that there would be such great difficulty in obtaining the medicine, he would have begged and collected some money from the villagers. Poor Panditji stood there helpless and perturbed, thinking about what he should do now. Suddenly the doctor came out of the bungalow. Panditji leapt and fell at his feet and spoke in a pitiful voice, 'O friend of the fallen! Three men of my house are sick with the plague. I am very poor, Sir. Please give some medicine.'

The doctor was used to such poor people coming to him every day. Someone falling at his feet or crying and prostrating himself before him was nothing new. If he showed compassion on this scale, then his own worth would be reduced to that of the medicines. Where, then, would all the luxury come from? However evil, though, he was at heart, he did talk sweetly. Pulling back his feet, he said, 'Where is the patient?'

Panditji told him, 'They are at home, Sir. How could I get them so far?'

The doctor expressed irritation. 'The patient is at home and you have come to get the medicine? How funny! How can I prescribe a remedy without seeing the patient?'

Panditji realized his mistake. How *could* the disease be diagnosed without seeing the patient? But it was not easy to get all the three patients so far. If the villagers helped, palanquins could be arranged. But here he had to accomplish everything on his own strength. There was no hope of getting help from the villagers. Let alone extending any help, they behaved as if they were his enemies. They feared that the rascal was going to invite some calamity by escalating confrontation with the gods. If it had been some other man, they would have killed him long ago. They, however, had developed affection for Panditji, which is why they had spared his life.

Although Panditji did not have the audacity to say anything further after hearing the doctor's response, he gathered himself and said, 'Sir, can nothing be done now?'

The doctor informed him, 'You can't get medicine from the hospital. I can give some from my own stock but that will be charged.'

Panditji asked, 'How much will this medicine cost, Sir?'

The doctor told him the price—ten rupees—and added that this medicine would be more beneficial than the one from the hospital. He said, 'There the medicine is old. The poor go there and get the medicine. Whoever is destined to live lives; whoever is destined to die dies. None of my concern. The medicine I will give you is the real thing.'

Ten rupees! At that moment, ten rupees seemed equivalent to ten lakh rupees to Panditji. Although he was used to spending such amounts every day on hemp and weed, now he was desperate for just a dime. He had no hope of getting credit from anyone. Although it was possible that begging, of course, might get him something, there was no way he could get ten rupees so quickly. For half an hour,

The Mantra

he stood there in confusion. He could not think of any way other than begging but he had never had the occasion to beg. Of course, he had collected donations, even thousands on a single round, but this was different. There was a singular pride in collecting donations as a protector of the faith, a servant of the community and a rescuer of Dalits. Accepting donations was a favour done to donors. But here he must stretch out his palm like beggars, must plead and bear insults. Someone might taunt, 'You are so healthy. Why don't you labour? Aren't you ashamed of begging?' Someone else might say, 'Go cut some grass. I will give you a good wage.' Nobody would believe him to be a Brahmin. If only he had his silk coat and his turban with him, or even a saffron scarf, he could pull off an act. He could pretend to be an astrologer and entrap any rich merchant, and he was anyway quite accomplished in that art. But here he had none of this. Even all his clothes had been robbed. If he stood in a field and delivered a delightful speech, then perhaps he would get a few devotees but this did not occur to him at all because when adversity strikes, even the brains get stunted. He could prove the magic of his words from a podium in an ornate enclosure standing in front of a desk decorated with flowers. But who would listen to his speeches when he was in such a terrible condition? People would think it was the gibberish of a madman.

The afternoon, however, was fading. There was no time for much deliberation. If it got late and dusk fell, it would be impossible to return at night. Who knows what might happen to the patients then? He could not wait in that state of indecision any more. There was no way other than begging, no matter how much he was humiliated or how much insult he would have to tolerate.

He reached the marketplace and stood in front of a shop but could not gather enough courage to beg for anything. The shopkeeper asked, 'What do you want?'

Panditji replied, 'What's the going rate for rice?'

At the next shop, however, Panditji turned more cautious. The trader was seated on a mattress. Panditji stood before him and recited a hymn from the Bhagavad Gita. The rich trader, amazed at his clear intonation and sweet voice, inquired, 'Where are you from?'

Panditji told him, 'I have come from Kashi.'

Panditji then proceeded to explain the ten signs of dharma and elaborated so well on the hymn that the trader was captivated. He requested, 'Sir, please accept my invitation and grace my house with your presence.'

A selfish man would have readily accepted the proposal but returning to the village was a more pressing concern for Panditji. He declined, saying, 'No, Sir, I do not have the time.'

The trader persisted with his request. 'Sir, you must grant me at least this much.'

When the trader could not get Panditji to agree to stay, he became pensive and said, 'Then how may I serve you? Command me. Your voice was not enough to satiate me. Should you arrive here again, bless me with your presence.'

Panditji answered, 'If you respect me so much, I will surely come.'

He then stood up, his lips having been sealed by hesitation. He thought, *The respect and welcome was extended only because I concealed my selfish motives. His eyes will turn away as soon as I express any want. Maybe he will not reject it outright, but there will be no more respect.* He descended the steps and stood on the street for a moment, pondering, *Where can I go now?* Meanwhile, the winter day was fading like the wealth of a debauchee. He was getting frustrated with himself. *Unless I beg from somebody, why would anyone give me anything? Does anyone know my heart? Gone are the days when rich men worshipped Brahmins. I must quit the hope that some good man will come and place the money in my hands.* He proceeded with slow steps.

Suddenly, the trader called after him, 'Panditji, please wait.' Panditji stopped, thinking, *Surely he is coming to request me once again to visit his house. Why could he not have brought a one-rupee note? Wonder what he wants from me at home.*

But when the trader actually placed a gold coin at his feet, Panditji's eyes welled up with tears of gratitude, and he said to himself, 'Really? The world still has real saintly men, otherwise would this earth not sink into the abyss?' At this moment, even if he had been asked for a litre or two of his own blood for the trader's well-being, he would have given it gladly. With his throat overwhelmed with happiness, he said, 'This was not required, Sir! I'm not a monk! I'm your servant.'

The trader replied politely and respectfully, 'My lord, please accept this. This is not charity, but a gift. Even I can tell a man's character. Many mendicants, hermits and servants of the nation and the faith keep visiting, but I don't know why my heart never feels any devotion for them. Getting rid of them becomes my only concern. I sensed from your hesitation that this is not your profession. You are learned and holy but in the midst of a crisis. Accept this lowly gift and bless me.'

7

When Panditji left for the village after collecting the medicines, his heart was jumping with joy, celebration and victory. Even Lord Hanuman would not have been so happy at finding the *sanjivani* herb. Panditji had never experienced such true happiness. His heart had never felt such lofty emotions.

Very little of the day was left. The sun god was running to the west with unstoppable speed. Was He too running to give medicine to some patient? Running with great speed, He hid behind a hill. Panditji picked up his pace, as if he was determined to catch up with the sun god.

Darkness fell very soon, and a star or two became visible in the sky. The destination was still ten miles away. Just as a housewife, upon seeing dark clouds, rushes to retrieve goods spread out for drying, Leeladhar too started running. He was not scared of travelling alone but of straying from the path because of the darkness. On both sides of the road, he was quickly leaving behind several hamlets. At this hour, Panditji found these villages to be balmy. He noticed the great pleasure with which people were warming themselves around bonfires.

Suddenly, he spotted a dog. God knows where he came from and how he came to be walking on the trail ahead of him. Panditji was startled but in a moment he recognized the dog. He was Moti, the old Chaudhuri's dog. Panditji said to himself, 'How has he come out so far from the village today? Does he know that I am coming with medicines and does not want me to lose my way? Who is the knowledgeable one here?' When he called out 'Moti' just once, the dog wagged his tail but did not halt. He did not want to waste time introducing himself. Panditji realized that God was with him and it was He who was protecting him. Now he was confident of reaching home safely.

Panditji reached home just as the clock was about to strike ten.

The illness was not fatal but it was Panditji's fortune to be of help. Three weeks later, all three patients recovered. Panditji's fame spread far and wide. He had rescued these men by waging a fierce battle against Yama, the god of death. He had achieved victory even over the gods. He had proved that the impossible could be made possible. He himself was now looked upon as God. People now came from far and wide to see him, but Panditji did not derive as much pleasure from his fame as from seeing the patients walk around in health.

The Chaudhuri said to him, 'Sir, you truly are God. We could not have survived had you not come here.'

Panditji replied, 'I didn't do anything. It is all God's mercy.'

The Chaudhuri said, 'Now we will never let you leave. Go get your wife and children also.'

Panditji agreed, 'Yes, I am of the same opinion. Now I can't leave you and go from here.'

8

Having found the battlefield vacant, the mullahs had been exercising great influence in the nearby villages. Village after village was converting to Islam. Meanwhile, the Hindu

Sabha had also withdrawn. No one was courageous enough to venture this way, though sitting afar, people were firing ammunition at Muslims. How to avenge Panditji's murder was their gravest concern. Officials were being regularly petitioned that the matter be investigated and the response was always that the assassins had not been traced. The collection for Panditji's memorial also continued unabated in the meantime.

But this new light left the mullahs pale. A god who could resurrect the dead, who could sacrifice his own life for the welfare of his devotees, had incarnated in the village. This accomplishment, this potion, this miracle was not available to the mullahs. How could vacuous arguments of paradise or fraternity counter such glowing beneficence? Even Panditji was now not the same Panditji who had been arrogant about his caste and learning. He had learned to respect the Shudras and the Bhils. Embracing them did not make Panditji cringe any more. It was only when they had found darkness at home that they had turned to the Islamic light. Now that their own houses were flushed with the light of the sun, why would they need to go elsewhere? Sanatan dharma emerged victorious. Temples were being built in every village and conch shells and bells could be heard at dawn and dusk in these temples. People's conduct started changing on its own. Panditji did not make anyone pure. Now even the name of the ritual, shuddhi, embarrassed him. He questioned himself, *What purification can I accord to them? Let me first purify myself. I cannot insult such pure and sacred souls with the pretence of shuddhi.*

This was the mantra that he learned from the Chandals and it was through the power of this mantra that he achieved success in protecting his own religion.

Panditji is still alive, but now he lives with his whole family in that very province, with those very Bhils.

Translated from the Hindi by Vikas Jain

The Lashes of Good Fortune

1

Boys, whether rich or poor, are known to be particularly cheerful. Their playfulness does not depend on wealth or familial circumstances. Nathua's parents were dead and the orphaned boy was usually found hanging about Rai Bholanath's gates. Rai Sahib was a compassionate man and, occasionally, he would give Nathua the odd paisa. Enough food was left over in Rai Sahib's kitchen to fill the stomachs of many orphans like him. Now and then, Nathua was also handed old clothes belonging to the boys in the family. So, even though he was an orphan, Nathua was not unhappy. Rai Sahib had rescued him from the clutches of a Christian. He did not care about the fact that Nathua would get some material comfort and schooling at the Mission; his only concern was that Nathua remain a Hindu. To him, the leftovers of his house were more blessed than the freshly cooked meal at the Mission. Sweeping his many rooms was better than getting schooled by the Christians. He must remain a Hindu, in whichever condition. If he turned Christian he would be lost forever.

Nathua had no other work except for cleaning Rai Sahib's bungalow. After his meal he played around the whole day. Nathua's work decided his position in the caste hierarchy and he was assigned a place in the sweeper community. Therefore, the other servants called him an untouchable, a *bhangi*, but he didn't mind. The poor boy was not aware of the effects this name could have on him and he saw no harm in being a bhangi. While sweeping, he often found some money or other things on the floor with which he could buy cigarettes. Even as a child he had acquired a taste for tobacco, cigarettes and paan in the company of other servants.

There were many boys and girls in Rai Sahib's household, for dozens of nieces and nephews lived with him. But he had only one daughter, whose name was Ratna. She was educated at home by two tutors and a British woman who came to teach her English. It was Rai Sahib's ardent desire that Ratna be accomplished and skilled so that, like the Goddess Laxmi, she would bring prosperity and fortune into her husband's home. He did not allow Ratna to mingle with the other children. She was given two rooms to herself—one to study in and the other to sleep.

People say that too much affection makes children wilful and naughty. But, in spite of being pampered, Ratna was well behaved and decent. She did not call the servants 'hey you' haughtily. She was not even rude to a beggar. She gave money and sweets to Nathua and sometimes also chatted with him. So the servant boy had become quite free and informal with her.

One day Nathua was sweeping Ratna's bedroom while she studied with the English memsahib in the other room.

As he swept the floor, an unfortunate thought came to him: He longed to lie on Ratna's bed. How clean and white the sheet was, how soft and cushioned the mattress and how beautiful the shawl! Ratna slept so cosily in the bed, just like chicks in a nest. That was why her hands were so soft and fair. It seemed as though her body was filled with cotton wool. Who will see me here, he thought to himself, and wiping his feet on the floor he quickly climbed into the bed and covered himself with the shawl. His heart filled with pride and joy. He happily jumped on the bed two or three times. He felt as though he lay cushioned on soft downy cotton. His body sank a finger's length into the mattress as he turned from one side to the other. Oh! Why is such joy not meant for me? Why didn't God make me Rai Sahib's son? These thoughts troubled Nathua and he sorely felt his own privation in the soft comfort of Ratna's bed. Just then Rai Sahib happened to come into the room. His eyes immediately fell on Nathua lying on Ratna's bed. Incensed, he shouted, 'Why, you pig, what are you doing?'

Nathua was petrified; he felt as though he had lost his foothold and toppled into a river. He leapt from the bed and snatched up his broom.

Rai Sahib asked again, 'What were you doing, wretch?'

'Nothing, master!'

'Are you brazen enough to sleep in Ratna's bed now? Ungrateful scoundrel! Bring me my whip.'

Rai Sahib flogged Nathua mercilessly. Nathua folded his hands and fell at Rai Sahib's feet but Rai Sahib's anger was implacable. All the servants crowded round and began to rub salt on his wounds. Rai Sahib's rage grew and throwing aside the whip he began to kick Nathua. When Ratna heard Nathua's cries she came running into the room. Once she had gathered the cause of the ruckus she pleaded with her father, 'Dadaji, the poor boy will die; have mercy on him now.'

Rai Sahib growled, 'If he dies, I'll have his carcass thrown out. At least he will have reaped the fruit for this wickedness.'

'It is *my* bed, isn't it? And I forgive him.'

'Just look at the state of your bed. The filth from the rascal's body must have rubbed off on it. What was he thinking? Why you . . . what came over you?'

Rai Sahib leapt at Nathua again but he ran and hid behind Ratna. There was no refuge elsewhere. Ratna stopped her father. 'Dadaji, I request you, please forgive him.'

Rai Sahib: 'What do you mean, Ratna? How can such villains be forgiven? All right, because of you I will let him go, otherwise I would have killed him today. You, Nathua, hear me, if you know what's good for you don't ever come here again. Get out right now, you no-good swine!'

Nathua ran for his life. He didn't look back even once and only stopped running when he reached the road. Rai Sahib could not touch him here. Here, people would not take Rai Sahib's side just to please him. Someone would be sure to speak up for him. After all, he was only a boy. Surely he couldn't be killed for making a mistake. Let him try and beat me here, he thought, I'll abuse him and run away. This idea bolstered his courage. He turned towards the bungalow and shouted, 'Come and hit me here, if you dare!' Then he took to his heels, in case Rai Sahib had heard him and was indeed coming after him.

2

Nathua had gone only a little distance when he saw Ratna's memsahib coming after him on her *tamtam*, the one-horse carriage. He was afraid she was chasing him to nab him. He fled at top speed once again but when he was too tired to run any further he had to stop. His mind said, *What can she do to me? What harm have I done her?* Meanwhile, the memsahib had reached him. Stopping her tamtam she said, 'Where are you going, Nathua?'

Nathua answered, 'Nowhere.'

'If you go back to Rai Sahib's he will beat you. Why don't you come with me to the Mission? You can live there comfortably and be educated and cultured.'

'Will you make me a Christian?'

'A Christian is not worse than a bhangi, silly!'

'No, Ma'am, I won't become a Christian.'

'Don't, if you don't want to. No one can force you to become one.'

Nathua went some distance in the tamtam but then suddenly he jumped down, for he was still suspicious of the Mission. The memsahib asked, 'What is it, why aren't you coming with me?'

'I've heard whoever goes to the Mission becomes a Christian. I won't go. You are tricking me.'

'Foolish boy, you'll be schooled there and not have to slave for anyone. In the evening you'll get time to play and have a coat and trousers to wear. At least come and see what it's like for a few days.'

Nathua did not respond to this temptation and ran down the alley. Only when the tamtam had gone quite far did he relax and begin to take stock of his situation. *Where do I go? I hope no policeman seizes me and takes me to the police station. If I go where people of my community live, will they take me in? Why shouldn't they? I won't just sit and eat; I will work and earn a living. I only need support, someone to stand behind me. If today I had someone to back me Rai Sahib would not have dared to beat me like that. The entire community would have rallied round and the whole house left uncleaned. Even the doorway would be unswept. Then, all his pride in his title would have been reduced to nothing.*

Having made up his mind. He wandered towards the bhangi quarter of the town. It was evening and many bhangis sat on mats under a tree playing the *shehnai* and the tabla. Music was their livelihood and they practised daily. The torment that music was subjected to here could not have happened elsewhere. Nathua went towards the players. A bhangi, who watched him listening very carefully, asked, 'Do you sing?'

Nathua replied, 'Not as yet, but if you teach me I will.'

'Don't make excuses, sit down; first let's hear you sing something and find out whether you have a good voice or not, otherwise how can one teach you?'

Like all the boys of the bazaar, Nathua also knew how to sing a little. He often sang and hummed while walking on the road. So he promptly broke into song. The teacher, respectfully called the ustad, heard him and understood that the boy was not worthless. He asked Nathua, 'Where do you live?'

Nathua introduced himself and poured out his tale of misery. He not only found shelter there but also got the chance to grow in a way that raised him from the earth and catapulted him into the heavens.

3

Three years flew by. Nathua's singing became the talk of the town. Singing wasn't the only thing he excelled in; his talents were manifold. In addition to singing, he played the shehnai, pakhawaj, sarangi, tamboura, and sitar—and he was skilled in all. Even his teachers wondered at his amazing genius. It seemed as though he was merely honing what he already knew. People practise playing the sitar for as long as ten years and still fail to learn it but Nathua had mastered its strings in just one month. So many gems like Nathua are lost in the dust because they do not meet a person discerning enough to see their hidden brilliance.

Serendipitously, a music conference was organized at Gwalior one day. Distinguished musicians from the country and abroad were invited. Nathua's teacher Ustad Ghurey also received an invitation. Nathua was his student. The ustad took Nathua along with him to Gwalior. The celebration went on for a week there. Nathua earned a lot of fame at the conference. He won a gold medal. The chairman of the music school of Gwalior requested Ustad Ghurey to admit Nathua into his music school. He would be taught music at the school and be educated as well. Ghurey consented and Nathua agreed to study there.

In five years Nathua had earned the highest degree of the school. Apart from music, he also showed proficiency in language, mathematics and science. He now had an honourable place in society. No one asked him his caste any more. His lifestyle, habits and demeanour were not of the low-caste singers but of an educated and genteel person. To safeguard his dignity be began to behave like high-caste people. He gave up meat and drink and took to regular puja. Not even a high-born Brahmin could have observed custom and conduct as he did. He was already known as Nathuram; now his name was further refined to N.R. Acharya. Often, he was simply called 'acharya', the learned and accomplished one. The acharya was also addressed as 'mahashay', or gentleman. Furthermore, the royal court began to give him a good salary. Very rarely does a talented man achieve such fame at the age of eighteen. However, the thirst for fame is never quenched. It is akin to the thirst of Rishi Agastya who drank up the ocean and was still not sated. The acharya also wanted to excel in Western music. He enrolled in the best music school of Germany and after five years of unrelenting labour and hard work he earned a master's degree. He toured Italy before returning to Gwalior and within one week of his arrival he was appointed by the Madan Company as inspector of their branches, with a monthly salary of three thousand rupees. Before going to Europe he had already made thousands of rupees. In Europe, too, the opera houses and theatres had welcomed him magnanimously and on some days he had earned more than a singer back home made in years. On his return the acharya was drawn towards Lucknow and decided to settle there.

4

When Acharya Mahashay reached Lucknow he was overwhelmed with emotion. He had spent his childhood here—he remembered how, as an orphan, he used to rob the square kites in these very alleys, and how he had gone begging in these bazaars. Ah! He was flogged here—he still carried the stripes of the whipping on his body. But now he held these scars dearer than the lines of fortune. In fact, for him the strokes of the whip had been a boon from Shiva.

There were no feelings of anger or revenge for Rai Sahib in his heart, not even a jot. He only remembered Rai Sahib's goodness; and he remembered Ratna as the very image of kindness and affection. For misfortune deepens old wounds, but fortune fills them up! The acharya alighted from the train with a palpitating heart. The ten-year-old boy had grown into a twenty-three-year-old learned and gracious young man. Now, not even his mother could have known him as her own Nathua. However, his transformation was considerably less amazing than the metamorphosis of the town. This was not Lucknow, but another city altogether!

As he emerged from the station his eyes fell on the people of the town, the prominent as well as the ordinary, waiting to welcome him. One of them was a beautiful young woman who resembled Ratna. The men shook his hand while Ratna garlanded him. This gracious welcome was accorded to him for bringing fame to Bharat in distant lands. The acharya's legs began to tremble; he found it difficult to stand still. This was the same Ratna! The innocent girl-child had taken the form of the Goddess of beauty, modesty, pride and grace. He did not have the courage to look straight into her eyes.

After the courtesies he was taken to the bungalow prepared for him. He was startled when he saw that it was the same mansion where he used to play with Ratna; the furnishings were the same, the pictures, chairs, tables and the gleaming mirrors were all the same . . . even the floor was unchanged. Acharya Mahashay stepped into the house with the same feelings a devout Hindu has when he enters a temple. As soon as he reached Ratna's bedroom his heart was so convulsed that tears began to flow from his eyes—this was the same bed, the same bedding and the very same floor! 'Whose bungalow is this?' he asked giddily.

The manager of the company was with him. He answered, 'One Rai Bholanath's.'

'Where did Rai Sahib go?'

'God alone knows where he went. The building was attached after he went bankrupt and was put up for auction. It was close to the theatre so I wrote to the authorities and bought it for the company. We got the fully furnished bungalow for forty thousand rupees.'

'You got it for free! Have you no news of Rai Sahib?'

'I heard that he had gone on a pilgrimage. God knows whether he has returned or not.'

In the evening Acharya Mahashay sat warily among the people who had called on him and asked one of those gathered, 'Do you have any news of Ustad Ghurey? I've heard a lot about him.'

The man answered sadly, 'Don't ask about him, master. He was returning home drunk when he fell unconscious on the road in front of a passing lorry. The driver didn't see him and he was crushed to death. His body was found in the morning. He was a rare musician, sir, and Lucknow became desolate with his death. Now there is no one in whom Lucknow can take pride. He had taught some of his art to a boy called Nathua and we had hoped he would keep the name of the ustad alive. But he went away to Gwalior and after that we don't know what happened to him.'

Acharya Mahashay was half-dead with the fear of being discovered. He could hardly breathe with the sword of Damocles hanging over his head. Fortunately, the moment finally passed and the clay pitcher remained whole even after being struck.

5

Acharya Mahashay lived in the house as gingerly as a new bride in her in-laws' home. The old values would not be erased from his heart. His self would not accept the fact that it was his house now. If he laughed out loud he would pull himself short with a start. If his friends who visited became too boisterous he would be engulfed by an unknown misgiving. If he were to sleep in the study, he would stay awake the whole night, for it was marked in his mind that the room was meant only for reading and writing. He could not change the old furnishings as they were still in fine shape. And, he never again opened Ratna's bedchamber. It remained shut and untouched. His legs trembled at the idea of entering the room, and the thought of sleeping on that bed never once crossed his mind.

The Acharya displayed the marvel of his musical genius many times at the Lucknow University. He would not sing at the households of kings and nobility even if they offered him lakhs of rupees. This he had vowed not to do. Those who were fortunate enough to hear his heavenly music were said to experience divine joy.

One morning Acharya Mahashay had just finished his puja when Rai Bholanath came calling. Ratna was also with him. Acharya Mahashay was overawed. His heart had not quaked like this even in the big and splendid theatres of Europe. He bent over double to greet Rai Sahib with a salaam. Bholanath was a little bewildered by this humility. It had been a long time since people had bowed to him. Now, wherever he went he was only mocked and derided. Ratna was also discomfited. Rai Sahib looked around him dejectedly and said, 'You must like this place.'

'Yes, sir, I cannot imagine a better place than this.'

'This is my bungalow. I had it made and I ruined it myself.'

Ratna said uncomfortably, 'Dadaji, what is the point of talking about this now?'

'There is no advantage, daughter, and no loss either. The mind is calmed by sharing one's grief with honourable men. Mahashay, this is my bungalow or, let me say, it was. I had an income of fifty thousand rupees a year from my estate but in the company of some men I began to gamble. At first, I quickly won two or three rounds. I was emboldened and began to wager and make lakhs of rupees. But a single loss destroyed everything and the chariot of my fortune floundered. All my property was ruined. Just think, twenty-five lakh was at stake. If the cowrie had only landed head-side up, the splendour of this bungalow would have been something else altogether! But it didn't and now I can only remember the days gone by and wring my hands in misery. My Ratna adores your singing and always talks of you. She has done her BA.'

Ratna flushed with embarrassment. 'Dadaji, Acharya Mahashay knows all about me. There is no need for this introduction. Forgive us, Mahashay, the bankruptcy has unsettled my father's mind. He came to ask you if you would mind his coming to see the bungalow occasionally. It would relieve his sorrow. He would be satisfied in the knowledge that a friend owns the house. We've come to you with only this request.'

The acharya replied humbly, 'You don't need to ask me. This house is yours, come whenever you wish. In fact, if you want you can live here; I'll find another place for myself.'

Rai Sahib thanked him and left. After that day he began to come every two or three days to the mansion and sat there for hours. Ratna always accompanied him. Eventually, they began to visit every day.

One day Rai Sahib took Acharya Mahashay aside and asked, 'Pardon me, but why don't you call your wife and children here? Living alone must be difficult for you.'

'I am not married; nor do I want to marry.' His eyes were lowered while he said this.

'Why is that? What do you have against marriage?'

'No special reason, just a preference.'

'Are you a Brahmin?'

The acharya coloured. He said with some unease, 'Caste differences do not matter after one travels to Europe. Whatever I may be by birth, my vocation makes me a Shudra.'

'Your humility is praiseworthy. It is truly remarkable that there are worthy people like you in this world. I also believe that deeds determine caste. Modesty, virtue, courtesy, good conduct, devotion, love for knowledge—these are all qualities of a Brahmin and I take you to be one. A person who does not have these characteristics is not a Brahmin, most certainly not. My Ratna feels great love for you. Till today no one has appealed to her but, forgive my being forward, you have bewitched her. Your parents—'

'You are my mother and my father. I don't know who gave birth to me. I was very young when they passed away.'

'Oh! If they were alive today their chests would have swelled immensely with pride. Where does one find such worthy sons as you?'

Just then Ratna came into the room with a paper in her hand. She said to Rai Sahib, 'Dadaji, Acharya Mahashay also writes poetry; see, I brought this from his table. Apart from Sarojini Naidu, I've not seen such good poetry elsewhere.'

The acharya stole a glance at Ratna and then said bashfully, 'These are just a few lines I scribbled. What would I know about writing poetry?'

6

Both the acharya and Ratna were desperately in love. Ratna was enamoured of his virtues and he was smitten with her. If Ratna had not crossed his path again, perhaps he would have never known love! But, once met, who can be indifferent to the alluring arms of love? Where is the heart that love cannot win?

Acharya Mahashay was drowned in uncertainty. His heart told him that the moment Ratna discovered his true identity she would turn her face away from him forever. No matter how generous she may be, or how painful she considered the chains of caste, she could not possibly be free of the aversion that would naturally arise towards him. So he did not have the courage to reveal his true self to her. Ah! If it were only a matter of revulsion he would not have hesitated, but the truth would cause her further grief, pain, heartbreak and there was no telling what she might do in the situation. To strengthen the ties of love while keeping her in the dark seemed to him the highest level of deceit. This was insincerity, trickery, villainy, and it was entirely unacceptable by the mores of love. He did not know what to do—he was caught in a terrible dilemma. On the one hand, Rai Sahib's visits became increasingly frequent and his heart's desire was reflected in his every word. On the other hand, Ratna began to come less often and this made Rai Sahib's wish still more evident. Three or four months passed like this. Acharya Mahashay would think, *He whipped me and turned me out of the house for lying on Ratna's bed for a few moments. When he finds out that I am the same orphan, untouchable, homeless boy, how much more anguish, self-mortification, humiliation, remorse and dismay it would cause him! How overcome would he be with remorse and the agony of a vain hope!*

One day Rai Sahib said, 'We should set a date for the wedding. During this auspicious period I want to be free of the debt of a daughter.'

'What date?' asked Acharya Mahashay, though he understood perfectly what Rai Sahib was talking about.

'Of Ratna's wedding. I don't care for matching horoscopes but the ceremony should be held at an auspicious time.'

The acharya kept his eyes glued to the ground and said nothing.

'You are familiar with my situation. I have nothing to give except my daughter. For whom should I have saved when I have no one else besides her?'

Acharya Mahashay was lost in thought.

'You know Ratna well. There is no need to praise her to you. Worthy or not, you must accept her.'

Acharya Mahashay's eyes overflowed.

'I firmly believe that God brought you here only for her. I pray to Him to bless you with a happy life. Nothing would make me happier. After fulfilling this duty I intend to spend my time in devotion to God, the rewards of which will also come to you.'

The acharya said in a choked voice, 'Sir, you are like my father but I am not at all worthy of this.'

Rai Sahib embraced him. 'Son, you possess all the virtues. You shine like a jewel in this society. It is a great honour for me to have you as my son-in-law. I will go now and see to setting the date and other things and inform you about them tomorrow.'

Rai Sahib stood up to go. The acharya wanted to say something but he did not have the opportunity or, shall we say, the courage to say it. His spirit was not so strong; nor did he have the power to bear Rai Sahib's loathing.

7

It had been one month since the wedding. Ratna's advent had lit up her husband's home and sanctified his heart. The lotus had blossomed in the sea.

It was night. Acharya Mahashay was lying down after his dinner—on the very bed that had caused him to be driven out of this house. The bed that had changed the wheel of his fortune.

For a month he had been searching for an opening to tell Ratna the truth. His soul refused to accept that his good fortune was the reward of his own virtues. He strove to dissolve the metal of his person in the furnace of truth to determine its real worth. But he could never find the occasion because as the moment he set his eyes on Ratna he became spellbound. Who goes to a garden to cry; a small, dark room suffices for that.

Just then Ratna came smiling into the room. The light of the lamp dimmed.

The acharya smiled and asked, 'Shall I put out the lamp?'

Ratna answered, 'Why, are you feeling shy?'

'Yes, actually I am.'

'Because I won you over?'

'No, because I deceived you.'

'You do not have the power to deceive.'

'You don't know that. I've kept a huge secret from you.'

Ratna: 'I know everything.'

'Do you know who I am?'

'Yes, I've known for a long time. When both of us played in this garden, when I'd hit you and you would cry . . . I'd give you my half-eaten sweets and you jumped on them . . . I've loved you since then. Of course, at that time it was expressed as kindness.'

The acharya was astounded. 'Ratna, you knew and still—'

'Yes, because I knew. I probably wouldn't have otherwise.'

'This is that same bed.'

'And I've come into the bargain with it.'

The acharya embraced her and said, 'You are the Goddess of forgiveness!'

Ratna replied, 'I am your handmaid.'

'Does Rai Sahib also know the truth?'

'No, he doesn't. And don't ever tell him or he will kill himself.'

'I still remember those whip lashes.'

'My father has nothing left now with which to atone for that. Are you still not satisfied?'

Translated from the Hindi by Meenakshi F. Paul

From Both Sides

1

Pandit Shyamswaroop was a young lawyer from Patna. He was not like the jaded young lawyers of today who are seen in smart circles, and whose physical and intellectual abilities, and visible and secret strengths seem to be concentrated on their tongues. No, our Panditji was not one of those young men who had grown old mentally. He was full of life and vigour. Although frugal with his words, his heart and mind pulsed with vitality and his hands and feet were all the more active. Once he settled on a course of action he remained steadfast. Another noteworthy quality that he possessed was that he did not take up too many tasks at one time. Those who put their fingers into many pies do not achieve anything. Stupid people might expect a fellow who is a secretary of a dozen committees and the president of half a dozen societies to do something really worthwhile. No sensible person would expect much of such an individual. All his energy and ability would be dissipated in empty talk.

Panditji understood this very well. He started a small organization for the untouchables and devoted a small part of his income and time to this noble cause. In the evenings he returned from his office, took some snacks, picked up his bicycle and went off to the villages adjoining the town. There he was seen conversing with the Chamars or chatting with the Doms about their culture in their colloquial dialects. He had no qualms in taking their children in his arms and showing them affection. On Sundays or any other holiday, he organized magic shows. Within a year, his interest in their welfare and constant companionship had led to considerable improvements in the lives of the untouchables of the region. Eating the flesh of dead animals stopped completely; and alcoholism, though not completely eradicated, was on the decline. In fact, the sundry unpleasant incidents caused by drunkenness had definitely reduced—much to the chagrin of Hamid Khan, the police inspector.

Panditji's kindness strengthened his bond of fellowship with the untouchables. There were around three hundred wards in his district and the number of people from upper castes was no less than six thousand. With all of them, he shared a warm, fraternal bond. He joined them in their wedding celebrations and accepted offerings according to the custom. If a conflict arose, the complaint was often taken to him. It was impossible for Panditji to hear about someone's sickness and not visit him to inquire after his health. He had some knowledge of indigenous medicine. He personally attended to the sick and even offered money, if needed. Most often, his affection and sympathy would suffice. Such occasions didn't require money as much as an urge for community service. His firm commitment and constant efforts brought about a radical change in the community within a year. Their homes and huts, their food and clothes, their manners and demeanour, improved very much.

The most important thing to happen was that these people learnt to respect themselves. Some boorish zamindars tried to threaten him but when they found that he was a man on a mission, they backed off. Some nincompoops tried to involve the police in the matter. Hamid Khan, the police inspector, was ready to interfere, but the Doms and the Chamars had nothing to offer him. Panditji's bond with them strengthened with the passage of time. Finally, a time came when Panditji not only attended the wedding of their chief's daughter but also shared a meal with them.

2

Pandit Shyamswaroop's wife was Kolesari Devi. Like most Indian women, she loved her husband deeply. She wasn't very educated, but living with Panditji helped her develop an awareness of the issues that concerned the nation and culture. She had just one weakness—she didn't have much patience for people's comments and opinions. She was not one with a very sharp tongue and she didn't make a fuss about every little thing. But a snide remark or a sardonic comment left her deeply troubled. She lent a patient ear to whatever was said to her and did not answer back. But she had a habit of nurturing grievances in her mind. Panditji knew about this and refrained from saying anything that would hurt her. He learnt this many years ago when, in the early years of his law practice, his income was meagre and expenses had to be balanced every day.

On the day of *sankranti*, Kolesari was generous enough to distribute five rupees worth of khichri to the poor. After spending the entire day without work at the court, when Panditji returned home empty-handed, he was annoyed to see the state of things.

He said harshly, 'I have to wander about and work hard for every single penny and here you are squandering money on unnecessary things. If this is what you wanted to do, you should've asked your father to marry you to a king or an emperor.'

Kolesari heard him out silently, her head down. She didn't retort, complain or shed tears. But she fell sick with fever and liver troubles for six months. Panditji had learnt the lesson of a lifetime.

He returned home after having a meal with Ramphal Chaudhary and, within moments, the news spread all over the town. The next day, Kolesari went to take a dip in the Ganga. It was probably the *Somwari Amavas*. Women from other well-to-do families had also come to take a dip. When they saw Kolesari, they began to whisper among themselves and gesture at her. One of them, who appeared to come from a rich family, said to the women next to her, 'Just take a look at this queen! Her husband goes about breaking bread with the Chamars and she comes to bathe in the Ganga.'

Kolesari overheard this. In fact, it was meant for her ears. Just as the potter's string pierces the clay, a harsh comment pierces the heart. Kolesari was deeply disturbed. She felt as though someone had driven a sharp knife into her heart. She forgot about the bath in the Ganga, retraced her steps and returned home. It was as if a snake's poison coursed through her body. She fed Panditji who left for the court. He had received a brief from a rich client that day. Excited at the prospect, he did not pay attention to his wife's changed mood. In the evening, when he returned home happy, he found her lying in bed with her head covered. He asked her, 'Kola, why are you lying in bed at this hour? Are you all right?'

Kolesari quickly sat up and said, 'I'm fine, I was just resting.'

But this answer did not convince Panditji. If she was fine, where was the red of the paan on her lips? Why was her hair dishevelled? Why this forlorn look on her face? Why had she not ordered ice for him? These thoughts ran through Panditji's mind.

He changed, ate a snack, chatted about his daily affairs, even cracked a couple of jokes. But these mantras did not mitigate the poison of the snake. Kolesari merely shook her head to whatever he said. The poison had shut her ears to everything. It was evening when Panditji went out for a spin. He took his bicycle and set off. But Kolesari's melancholic face haunted him. That day, there was a wedding of the Pasis in Maajh village. He went there.

The groom's party had come from a far-off village. They were asking for liquor be served to them; the girl's people flatly refused to oblige them. The groom's people also demanded that the women of the community dance at the doorstep to welcome them, as was the custom, and that the drum be beaten. The hosts said they did not follow this practice any more. Panditji's efforts had brought about a welcome change in Maajh village. The people from the groom's side were untouched by his influence. When Panditji reached the venue, he explained things to the guests and pacified them.

On such days, he would usually return home by nine or ten at night, as his counselling on such occasions had great impact. But today his heart was not in what he was doing. Kolesari's forlorn, withered face flashed before his eyes. He kept wondering whether he had said something that pained her. He couldn't remember any such thing.

'What is troubling her, then? There must be a reason.' Troubled by such thoughts, he returned home by seven o'clock.

3

Panditji ate his dinner and went to bed. Kolesari couldn't eat even a morsel. She was still looking glum. Finally, Panditji asked her, 'Kola, why are you so sad?'

'I'm not sad.'

'Are you all right?'

'Of course. I'm sitting before you hale and hearty.'

'I don't believe you. There must be some reason for your sadness. Don't I have a right to know?'

'You are my master. You certainly have the right to know before anyone else.'

'Then why this veil of secrecy between us? I don't keep any secrets from you.'

Kolesari lowered her eyes and asked, 'Do I hide things from you?'

'So far, you haven't, but today you're definitely hiding something from me. Look into my eyes. People say that women can gauge a man's love in an instant. Probably you haven't yet understood the depth of my love. Believe me, your melancholic face has made me restless the whole day. If you don't tell me now, I'll assume you don't trust me.'

Kolesari's eyes filled with tears. She looked at him and said, 'Will you remove the thorn that rankles my heart?'

Shyamswaroop was stung.

He sat up, filled with all kinds of apprehensions and managed to say tremulously, 'Kola, you are being unfair to me by asking such a question. I am yours and all that I have is yours. You shouldn't have any misgivings about me.'

Kolesari realized that she had said something she didn't mean, so she quickly corrected herself. 'God knows that I've never doubted your love. I asked the question because I thought when you know the reason for my sadness, you might laugh it off. I know that I shouldn't be saying this. I also know it'll hurt you deeply to agree to my request. That is why I wanted to hide my feelings from you. I would've forgotten all about it in a few months. But your entreaties have forced me to speak up. Do you realize what'll happen to me when you really believe that I don't trust you? It is your plea that is forcing me to speak.'

'Come on, tell me without fear. I can't bear the suspense any more.'

'Please stop mixing with the untouchables and eating with them.'

Just as an innocent prisoner, condemned by the judge, lets out a deep sigh, Panditji also heaved a deep sigh in total puzzlement and lay down on his bed silently.

Then he stood up and said, 'All right. I shall obey your order. My heart will bleed, but let that be. But tell me one thing, is this your idea or has someone put you up to it?'

'Women mock me. I cannot put up with this. I have no control over their tongues, they can say anything. But I have some rights over you, so I made the request.'

'All right. What you say will be done.'

'I have one more request to make. I've told you candidly what was in my heart. Men are not as bothered by people's jibes as women who are weak. Our hearts are weak; harsh comments affect us deeply. But don't pay attention to this. Don't be violent to yourself to protect me from people's taunts. I'll put up with them. If they hurt me too much, I'll stop going out and meeting these women.'

Shyamswaroop hugged Kolesari and said, 'Kola, I can't take it that you have to listen to people's taunts because of me. I won't allow your sensitive heart to be wounded by taunts. Should your heart be filled with pain, where would my love find shelter? Now, cheer up and sing me your favourite song.'

Kolesari's face lit up with joy. She picked up the harmonium and began to sing in a sweet melodious tone.

Piya milan hai kathin bawri . . .

Love's union is difficult, O my crazy heart . . .

4

A week passed and Panditji did not visit the villages. It was his life's mission to form a fraternal bond with the untouchables, to make them aware about their self-worth as human beings and to pull them out of the cesspool of ignorance and superstition. Whenever a spanner was thrown in the works, derailing his hopes, he was sad and distressed.

Human beings enjoy life as long as they feel they are doing something worthwhile. Of course, there are many in this world who do not know what their social or personal responsibilities are. But then it is wrong to call such people humans. Those who become accustomed to doing wrong things cannot refrain from them, even if they know what they are doing is wrong. And if fair means are not available, they take recourse to foul means to get what they want. You may warn or threaten a gambler as much as you want but he won't give up playing the game. You may throw a drunkard in prison, but the moment he is set free he will rush to the pub. Wicked deeds have their own excitement. But the passion for doing good excites one many times over. His daily chores would keep Panditji occupied through the day but, come evening, when it was time for the activities closer to his heart, he felt restless. He had to be violent to his true self by giving preference to his personal duty over his social responsibility. When he sat alone in the evening in his little garden, he would argue with himself. At times, he became terribly annoyed at his own helplessness and felt like walking up to Kolesari and telling her firmly that he couldn't sacrifice the good of the community for personal interest.

'But what will be the effect of these words on Kola? She is a simple, innocent soul, blind in her love for me. Won't it pain her deeply? *No, Kola, I love you more than my life. You who are so precious to me, how can I think of myself as unfortunate when I have you? I will bear everything to keep you happy. If only you knew how restless I was right now, I am sure you won't care about people's jibes. No, you won't care even if all the people in the whole world pointed their fingers at you. What can I offer you in return for your unwavering love?* The duty towards one's community is perhaps the highest of all obligations. However, in special circumstances, sometimes one has to abandon the community to maintain domestic peace. It was the duty of King Ramachandra to stay back in Ayodhya and be a just ruler to his people, ensuring peace and prosperity. But for him, his father's command took precedence, which was a personal duty. It was also the duty of King Dasharath to hand over the throne to Rama who was loved by the people of Avadh. But he abandoned this national duty to honour a personal vow that he had made.'

Pandit Shyamswaroop, however, was wrong in assuming that Kolesari was unaware of the struggle in his heart. Since the night she had brought up the issue, she was constantly haunted by the thought that she had been unfair to him. She could see that his face did not reflect joy and contentment, as it did before. He didn't show the same interest in his food and drink. His conversations barely concealed the pain in his heart. Kolesari could see what was happening to him as clearly as her reflection in a mirror.

She reproached herself. 'How selfish I am! How can I allow myself to be affected by a low, ill-tongued and shallow woman as to be so unfair to my husband? He has endured so much for my sake and I was affected by a mere taunt?'

These thoughts made her feel she must free him from the vow that he had taken. But Panditji didn't give her any opportunity to bring up the issue.

5

Pandit Shyamswaroop's untouchable brothers waited for him for a week. 'Maybe he's unwell,' they thought, 'or busy in a court case or out on vacation.' For a week, they kept themselves content with these thoughts. But after that, their patience ran out. Crowds of them descended on his home, wearing thick shawls, white turbans on their heads, feet shod in leather, and walking sticks on their shoulders. They wanted to know if all was well. Panditji had to offer an excuse for his absence and the only excuse he could think of at that moment was that his wife had been sick. From morning till evening, the stream of visitors continued unabated. As visitors from one village left, those from another would arrive. He had to offer the same excuse to all. He had no other option.

The second week passed but at Panditji's house the pretence of sickness continued. One evening, he was sitting at his doorstep when Ramdeen Pasi, Ballu Chaudhary and Gobari Pansphod arrived with Hakim Nadir Ali Khan in their tow. Hakim Sahib was the Ibn-e-Sina of his times. Just as Satan takes to his heels with the chanting of *ism-e aazam*, ailments, however chronic or complicated, vanished with Hakim Sahib's arrival. And sometimes, his patients vanished too.

Panditji was nonplussed to see Hakim Sahib. 'Now what trick should I play?' he thought to himself. 'I'll be completely exposed! What made these stupid fellows fetch this hakim here? And how on earth was this gentleman ready to come here like the angel of death?'

He was indeed in a fix and there was no time to mull over things. At that moment, despite his deep love for Kolesari, he wished that she indeed had fever. It would have helped him save face. But then, death never comes when one invokes it!

Hakim Sahib said, 'I was so sorry to hear that your esteemed wife has been sick for the last two weeks. I am unhappier with you, Sir, that you did not inform me of her illness. If you did, the sickness wouldn't have lasted so long. What is her complaint?'

Panditji scratched his head, coughed once or twice, changed his posture, lowered his head and replied, 'It's one of those women's problems, but she's much better now. A lady doctor is seeing her. You know very well how people are embracing Western culture. They have more faith in Western medicine. And then, you also know that patients show improvement if they have faith in the doctor and the mode of treatment. It is for this reason that I didn't think it proper to trouble you.'

'Yes, you're right. Which lady doctor is treating her?'

Panditji scratched his head again and replied, 'Miss Bogan . . .'

Shyamswaroop had to employ all his legal skills to deal with the situation. But it was clearly not a good day for him. The situation, instead of easing up, was becoming more complicated. Even as they were speaking, he saw Kallu Chaudhary, Hardas Bhar and Jugga Dhobi arriving in the company of Miss Bogan, who was riding a horse. Panditji became tense and all the colour drained from his face. In his heart he cursed Miss Bogan, wondering how she had landed there at that hour! But this was not the occasion to show his annoyance. He quickly rose from his chair, shook hands with Miss Bogan and, before she could utter a word, guided her to the sitting room in the women's section.

He then went up to Kolesari and said, 'We're stuck in a peculiar situation. I'd made a pretence of your sickness to get rid of these people. But today, they've brought over Hakim Nadir Ali Khan and Miss Bogan to treat you. Miss Bogan is sitting in the drawing room. Now tell me what to do.'

'Shall I pretend to be sick then?'

'May your enemies fall sick!' laughed Panditji.

'Even if they do, it won't help right now. You bring Miss Bogan. I'll get under the blanket.'

Panditji went to the sitting room to fetch Miss Bogan. In the meanwhile, Kolesari covered herself with a blanket from head to toe and started groaning as though she were in great pain. Miss Bogan checked her temperature with a thermometer, examined her tongue, made a face and said, 'The illness has taken deep root. It's hysteria. Apparently, there's no fever in your body, but you must be feeling it in your chest. You have a headache, don't you?'

'I feel as though my head will burst. There's an abscess.'

'You don't feel hungry, do you?'

'Can't even bear to look at food!'

Miss Bogan completed her diagnosis. She wrote down the prescription and left. Hakim Nadir Ali thought it futile to stay on any longer as he had already collected his fees.

Panditji came out and told his well-wishers, 'You have taken the trouble for no reason. She's much better now. I am very grateful to all of you.'

Once the guests had taken his leave, Panditji went inside and laughed to his heart's content. Then he thought to himself, 'Today, I had to do things that should never have been done. Won't the lady understand even now?'

But Kolesari found it difficult to laugh.

6

After his meal, Pandit Shyamswaroop went to bed and fell asleep, but Kolesari was unable to sleep. She kept tossing and turning. Sometimes she would stand up and start pacing up and down, or she would sit at the table in an effort to read a book in the light of the table lamp. But she couldn't set her mind to anything. Her thoughts rebounded like the rays of the moon streaming through a tree being buffeted by a storm.

She thought to herself—*How unfair I've been to him. What pain he must have gone through today. A man who has never uttered a lie in his entire life had to tell so many today! And all because of me! If he were accustomed to telling lies, we would be the owners of the vast Didarganj estate today! I've reduced a truthful man to such a plight! Is it for this that I am to share his destiny? It's my duty to support him, to assist him in his endeavours, to give him the right advice and see to it that he is at peace. Instead, I've trapped him in a web of lies. May God forgive my sins!*

It was my duty to assist him in his good deeds. These villagers are so simple, guileless and generous. I've stopped my husband from working for such good people! Why? Just because an ill-tongued woman made a jibe at me? I was so incensed that I forced him to lie! Despite my mean-spirited torments, my generous and pure-hearted husband has remained unchanged. He has been more virtuous than virtue, and more honest than honesty. He knows I'm silly and stupid, ignorant and weak and obstinate, yet he hides my follies and continues to love me. How narrow-minded I am! I'm not worthy of even washing his feet! Today, how he laughed when he returned after seeing Miss Bogan off. What a guileless laughter it was! Just to keep my spirits up and to mitigate my guilt. My love, I'm downright evil! I'm petty-minded. But please remember, I'm your slave . . .

As these thoughts ran through her mind, she turned to look at Pandit Shyamswaroop's face. It appeared content because of a restful sleep. A faint smile played on his lips. As she gazed at her husband, she felt a lump in her throat. Like the high tides in the sea, there are times when human hearts, too, experience the tide of love. At that moment, it seemed as if a river of love had welled up in Kolesari's eyes. Overwhelmed with emotion, she clung to his chest which contained deep love for her. Just as a thief plunders a house freely if the owner is asleep, Kolesari drew her husband's love. And just as a thief fears lest the owner wake up, she, too, was fearful of her husband waking up. A woman's love is restrained. A sense of shame stops her from being demonstrative. The fear that her enthusiasm might be construed as exhibitionist or phoney restrained her from an untrammelled expression of her love. But at that moment Kolesari was free from such fears. When the sea swells in high tide, the waves carry parts of damaged ships, scraps and shells to the shore. The tide of love in Kolesari's mind swept away all the fetters that had kept her bound for so long.

7

When Panditji returned home from the court the following day, he said to Kolesari, 'Can I have your permission to go out for a couple of days?'

'Why? Where are you going?'

'I've taken up a case outside the city. I've to go to Bhagalpur.'

'Right now?'

'The hearing is fixed for tomorrow.'

At six in the evening, Panditji left for Bhagalpur. The case kept him occupied for the next four days. He had promised to return in three days, but his work took four days. It was only on the fifth day that he was free of the case and, by three that afternoon, he reached Patna and made his way home. As he entered his neighbourhood, he ran into Sanpat Chaudhary of Maajh village.

He asked him, 'Chaudhary, where are you headed?'

Chaudhary looked up in surprise and replied, 'Greetings, Sir. Weren't you expected to return yesterday? What delayed you?'

'I couldn't make it yesterday. Is everything fine with you?'

'By your grace. A big event is going on at your place.'

'My place? What kind of event?' he asked in astonishment.

'Bahuji has arranged a get-together. All our women were invited.'

Filled with joy, Panditji proceeded towards his home. He encountered many familiar faces on the way. It seemed as though a lot of villagers had come to attend a wedding. After exchanging greetings with them he finally reached home and saw a huge crowd gathered there. Many guests were sitting on the floor and smoking hookahs. Kolesari had invited the women. These men had chaperoned their women.

Panditji went to the sitting room and changed his clothes. He instructed the servants to not tell anyone of his arrival. He took his position at the window and began to observe what was happening.

The inner courtyard was covered with clean white sheets and on them sat about three to four hundred village women, all dressed for the occasion. Some were laughing while others were chatting amongst themselves. He saw Kolesari distributing paan and cardamom on a platter among guests. After the distribution of paan, the singing began. Kolesari was wearing a simple sari of thick weave and no jewellery. She drummed the dhol and began singing along with the women. As Panditji watched this, his heart swelled with great joy. He felt like rushing to Kola and holding her close to his heart.

When the singing was over, Kola addressed the women for fifteen minutes in their colloquial language. After that, the women dispersed. Kolesari gave each one of them a warm hug before saying goodbye. One of the women was very old. When she came forward to receive the hug, Kolesari bent down to touch her feet to seek her blessings. Panditji was so thrilled by Kolesari's courtesy and humility that he actually jumped with joy a couple of times. Unable to restrain himself any longer, he left the sitting room and walked to the inner courtyard.

He called Kolesari into the room and took her in his arms.

She asked, 'Why were you delayed? Had you not returned today, I would've come to see what's wrong.' But Panditji had no time to listen to pleasantries.

He hugged her again and again.

Embarrassed, Kolesari said, 'That's enough. Do you want to expend all your love today?'

'What can I say? It does not seem enough to me. The more I love, the more I want to love you. You are truly a goddess.'

Maybe not a kingdom, but if Panditji had been given a large estate, he would not have felt the joy that he had experienced that day.

After showering his wife with affection, he stood in the courtyard and addressed the village women: 'Sisters, Kola was not sick. She had forbidden me to mix with all of you. But today, by inviting all of you, she's created the bond of sisterhood. I cannot describe in words the joy I feel at this moment. As an expression of my happiness, I've decided to open *kothi*s for transactions of loans in ten villages with the capital of a thousand rupees each. There, you'll be given loans free of interest. When you borrow from moneylenders you're made to pay an interest of one or two anna per rupee borrowed. With the opening of this facility, you'll be free from the clutches of the moneylenders. These kothis will be managed by the lady who's invited you all here today.'

The women raised their hands in appreciation and blessed Panditji. Kolesari said to her husband, 'You've given me such a great responsibility.'

'Now that you've stepped into the water, you'll soon learn to swim,' Panditji said, smiling.

'But do I know anything about keeping accounts and ledgers?'

'You'll learn automatically. Did you know how to counsel people? You were too shy to even speak to women. Only two weeks earlier, you forbade me to meet these people and today you're treating them as your sisters! You've had your way earlier, now it's my turn.'

'You set the net to trap me, didn't you?' laughed Kolesari.

'It's a trap we set for each other.'

Translated from the Urdu by M. Asaduddin

Witchcraft

1

Doctor Jaypal had received a first rank certificate but thanks to destiny or ignorance of professional principles he had never achieved prosperity in his career. His house was in a narrow alley but it didn't occur to him to get a house in an open area. The cupboards, jars and medical instruments in his pharmacy were quite grubby. In domestic matters, too, he was determinedly frugal.

His son had come of age but the question of his education had not yet arisen. *What great wealth have I gained banging my head against books for so long that I should waste thousands of rupees on his education*, he would think. His wife Ahalya was a patient lady but Doctor Sahib had put such a burden on these virtues of hers that her back too was bent. His mother was alive and would yearn for a chance to bathe in the Ganga; as for visiting other sacred sites, the subject never arose. Because of this severe thriftiness, there wasn't the least joy or peace to be found in the house. The happy odd man out was the old servant woman, Jagiya. She had nursed the infant Doctor Sahib and come to love the family so much that she withstood all manner of hardship but never considered going away.

2

To make up for the shortage of income from his practice, the doctor had shares in cloth and sugar factories. The Bombay factory had by chance that day sent him his annual dividend of seven hundred and fifty rupees. Doctor Sahib opened the insured parcel, counted the notes, and said goodbye to the postman. But the postman had too many rupee coins; he was sinking under the weight.

He said, 'Huzoor, I'd be much obliged if you took the coins and gave me the notes, it would lighten my load.'

Doctor Sahib used to keep the postmen happy and would give them free medicines. He thought, *Well, I'll anyway have to call a tonga to get to the bank, why don't I make a virtue of a necessity.*

He counted the rupee coins, put them in a purse and was just thinking that he should go deposit them in the bank when a patient sent for him. Occasions like these rarely arose. The doctor had no faith in the storage box but was helpless. He put the purse in it and went to see the patient. It was three o'clock when he returned and the bank had closed. There was no way the money could be deposited that day. Like every other day he took his place in the pharmacy.

At eight when he was about to go into the house, he brought out the purse to take with him and it felt somewhat lighter. He immediately weighed it on the scales he used for medicines and was stunned. It was a whole five hundred rupees less. He couldn't believe it. He opened the purse and counted the money. It did turn out to be five hundred rupees short. He agitatedly felt around the other compartment of the box but it was useless. Dejected, he sat down, closed his eyes in order to focus his power of recall, and started thinking. *Did I put part of the money elsewhere? Did the postman give me less? Did I make an error in counting it? I'd laid out piles of twenty-five rupees each and there were exactly thirty piles, I remember that well. I counted each pile and put it into the purse, my memory isn't fooling me. I remember everything clearly. I'd locked the box too but . . . oh . . . now I know, I left the keys on the table, in my hurry I forget to take them. They're still on the table. That's it—it slipped my mind to put the keys in my pocket. But who took them, the outside door was closed. No one touches money that's lying in the house; nothing like this has ever happened before. For sure this is the work of some outsider. It could be that one of the doors was left open, someone came in to get medicine, saw the keys on the table, and opened the box to lift out money.*

This is why I don't take rupees. Who knows, perhaps it's the postman's doing. It's very likely. He saw me putting the purse in the box. If I'd deposited the money I'd have a whole thousand rupees, it would have been easy to calculate the interest. What should I do? Should I inform the police? It'll be a needless complication. The people of the whole quarter will crowd at the door. Five or ten people will have to suffer abuses and there'll be no result. So then, should I stay put and keep calm? How to stay calm! This was no wealth I'd got gratis. If it was ill-gained money I'd say it's gone the way it came. But every coin I've earned with my sweat. Me, who lives so frugally, with so much hardship, who is renowned for his stinginess, cuts corners even on essential household costs—for what? So that I can amass goods for the enjoyment of some swindler? I don't hate silk, nor is fruit unappetizing, nor does cream give me indigestion, nor is the sight in my eyes dim that I can't enjoy the pleasures of the theatre and the cinema. I fence in my mind from all sides in order to have a few extra coins so that when they're needed I don't have to go begging. I could buy some property, or if not at least have a nice house made. But this is the result of my abstinence—the money made from hard-won effort looted. It's so unfair that I should be robbed like this in broad daylight and not a hair out of place on the head of that villain. It must be Diwali in his house, celebrations must be on, the whole lot of them must be blowing bugles.

Doctor Sahib started longing for revenge. *I've never let any fakir, any sadhu, stand at the door. Even though I wanted to, I've never invited my friends home; I've always stayed away from relatives and associates. For this? If I could find out who he is, I'd kill him with a poisoned injection.*

But there's no remedy. A poor weaver vents his anger on his beard. Even the intelligence bureau is just so in name, they're not capable of finding out. All their intelligence is expended in political speeches and writing false reports. I ought to go to someone who knows mesmerism; he'll be able to solve this problem. I've heard that in Europe and America robberies are often traced this way. But who is such a master of mesmerism here, and besides, the answers mesmerism gives are not always to be trusted. Like astrologers, they too start taking plunges in the endless ocean of guesswork and conjecture. Some people can divine names too. I've never believed in these stories but there's an element of truth in them for sure, otherwise in this day and age they wouldn't exist. Even today's scholars concede that there is something like spiritual power. But even if someone tells me the name, what means do I have at hand to take revenge? Inner knowledge won't suffice as evidence. Except for the moment's peace my heart will get, what else is to be gained from this?

Yes, I remember now. That sorcerer who sits near the river—I've heard stories about his feats. It seems he can trace stolen money, instantly make the sick well, locate stolen goods and cast spells. I've heard praises of that spell—the spell is cast and blood begins to spill from the thief's mouth. Till he returns the goods, the bleeding won't stop. If this meets its mark then my heart's desire is fulfilled. I'll get the outcome I want. The money is returned to me and the thief is taught a lesson! There's always a crowd at his place. If he isn't capable why would so many people congregate there? There is a glow on his face. Today's educated people don't have faith in these things, but among the lower classes and the society of the foolish there is a great deal of talk about him. Every day I hear stories about ghosts and spirits. Why don't I go to this sorcerer? Even if I don't gain anything what could be the harm? Where five hundred have gone, let two or four rupees more be squandered. The time is right. The crowd will be smaller, I should get going.

3

Having thus made up his mind, Doctor Sahib went towards the sorcerer's house. It was nine o'clock on a winter's night. The streets had almost emptied. The sound of the Ramayana being chanted was occasionally heard from the houses. After a while complete silence descended. There were fertile green fields on either side of the road. The wailing of jackals became audible. It seemed the pack was quite near. Doctor Sahib had generally had the good fortune to hear their melodious voices from afar. Not close up. Now, in this silence, to hear their shrieks from so near frightened him. He repeatedly knocked his stick on the ground and stamped his feet. Jackals are cowards; they don't come near human beings. But then he thought, If any one of them is mad, then his bite will be lethal. As soon as he thought of this the memory of germs, bacteria, Pasteur Institute and Kasuali began whirring in his head. He began to take hurried strides. Suddenly, it occurred to him—*What if someone from my own home has taken the money?* He immediately stopped but in a moment resolved this too. *There's no harm; in fact, the family should get even harsher punishment. I can have no compassion for the thief, but I have a right to the family's sympathy. They ought to know that whatever I do, I do for them. If I kill myself day and night it's for them that I kill myself. If despite this they're prepared to betray me then who could be more heedless, more ungrateful, more heartless than them? They should be punished severely. So severely, so instructively, that no one ever dares do something like this again.*

Eventually he arrived near the sorcerer's house. The lack of a crowd calmed him. But his pace had slowed down a little. He thought to himself again—*If all this turns out to be a complete fraud, I'll be needlessly shamed. Whoever hears will take me for a fool. Perhaps the sorcerer himself will consider me a fool. But now that I've come, let me try this. If nothing else, I'll have tried it.*

The sorcerer's name was Budh. People called him Chaudhuri. He was a tanner by caste. His house was small and dirty too. The thatch was so low that even stooping one was in danger of knocking one's head. There was a neem tree by the door. Beneath that an altar. A flag fluttered on the neem tree. On the altar were hundreds of clay elephants painted with sindoor. Several iron-tipped trishuls had been dug into the ground too and looked like they were spurring the sluggish elephants. It was ten o'clock. Budh Chaudhuri, a dark-complexioned, pot-bellied and commanding man, sat on a torn sackcloth drinking from a coconut. A bottle and a glass were before him.

As soon as he saw Doctor Sahib, Budh hid the bottle and, getting up, salaamed him. An old lady brought out a stool for him. With some embarrassment Doctor Sahib laid out the whole incident. Budh said, 'Huzoor, this is no big deal. Just this Sunday the police inspector's watch was stolen, several investigations undertaken but nothing found. They called me. I found out as we spoke. I got five rupees as reward. Yesterday the Corporal Sahib's horse went missing. He was running around in all directions. I gave him the address where the horse was found grazing. Thanks to these skills all the lords and masters trust me.'

The doctor was not interested in this talk about the inspector and the corporal. *Whatever they are in the eyes of these illiterates, they are merely an inspector and a corporal.* He said, 'I don't just want to get to the bottom of the robbery, I also want to punish the thief.'

Budh shut his eyes for a moment, yawned, snapped his fingers, then said, 'This is the work of somebody from the house.'

The doctor said, 'It doesn't matter, whoever it is.'

The old woman said, 'Later if anything goes amiss, huzoor will think ill of us.'

The doctor said, 'Don't you worry about that. I've given it a lot of thought. In fact, if this is the mischief of someone from the house then I want to be even stricter with them. If an outsider tricks me then he deserves pardon, but I could never forgive a family member.'

Budh said, 'So what does huzoor want?'

'Just that I get my money and misfortune strikes the thief.'

'Shall I cast the spell?'

The old woman said, 'No, son, don't go near the spell. Who knows which way it'll fall?'

The doctor said, 'You cast the spell, whatever the fee and reward, I'm willing to pay.'

The old woman said, 'Son, I'm saying it again. Don't go after the spell. If something dangerous happens and this same babuji harasses you again, you won't be able to remedy a thing. Don't you know how hard it is to reverse the spell?'

Budh said, 'Yes, Babuji! Think carefully one more time. I could cast the spell, but I don't take responsibility for undoing it.'

'Didn't I just say I won't ask you to undo it? Cast it now.'

Budh made a long list of the necessary items. The doctor thought it might be better to give him money instead of these things. Budh agreed. As he was leaving, the doctor said, 'Cast such a spell that by morning the thief is before me with the money.'

'Don't you worry,' Budh said.

4

It was eleven when the doctor took off from there. The winter night was bitterly cold. His wife and mother were both up, on the lookout for him. To while away the time they had put a brazier between them which affected their minds more than their bodies. Coal was an item of luxury for them. The old maid, Jagiya, lay nearby, huddled under a piece of torn matting. Now and again, she would get up and go into her small, dark room, feel around for something in the alcove and then return to lie down in her place. 'How late is it?' she'd ask repeatedly. She'd start at the slightest sound and look around her with worried eyes. It surprised everyone that the doctor was not back at his usual time. He rarely went out at night to see patients. Even if some people had faith in his treatment, they dared not enter this alley at night. And he had no taste for cultural clubs and societies, or for the company of friends.

His mother said, 'I wonder where he went, the food has gone completely cold.'

'If a person goes somewhere he informs and goes. It's past midnight,' said Ahalya.

'Something must have hindered him. Otherwise, when does he go out of the house?'

Ahalya said, 'I'm going off to sleep, he can return when he likes. Who's going to sit and keep watch all night?'

They were talking thus when Doctor Sahib returned. Ahalya stayed where she was; Jagiya stood up and stared at him in fear.

'Where were you held up for so long today?' his mother asked.

'You're all sitting pretty, aren't you! I am late but why should you care? Go, sleep happily, I'm not fooled by these superficial demonstrations. If you got the chance you'd cut my throat, and you're making an issue of this!'

Pained, his mother said, 'Son! Why do say these hurtful things? Who is your enemy in the house to think ill of you?'

'I don't consider anyone my friend; all are my enemies, the destroyers of my life. Otherwise, would five hundred rupees vanish from my table as soon as my back was turned? The door was bolted from outside, no stranger came in, the money disappeared as soon as I put it there. Why should I consider them mine, those who are thus bent on slitting my throat? I've found out everything, I'm just returning from a sorcerer. He clearly said it's the doing of someone in the house. It's fine—as you sow, so shall you reap. I'll show you how I'm no well-wisher of my enemies. If it was an outsider I'd perhaps have let him go but if the family for whom I toil day and night deceives me like this, they deserve no leniency. See what shape the thief is in by tomorrow morning. I've told the sorcerer to cast the spell. The spell is cast and the thief's life is at risk.'

Jagiya said agitatedly, 'Brother, a spell endangers life.'

'That's the thief's punishment.'

'Which sorcerer has cast it?' she asked.

'Budh Chaudhuri.'

'Arré Ram, there's no taking down his spells.'

When the doctor went into his room, his mother said, 'The devil eats the miser's wealth. Someone scavenged away five hundred rupees. For that amount I could have visited all seven *dhaam*s.'

Ahalya said, 'For years I've been fighting for bangles. Good thing it's my curse.'

'Who on earth will take his money in the house?'

'The doors must have been left open, some outside person made away with it.'

His mother said, 'How is he so certain that it's one of us who stole the money?'

'Greed for money makes a man suspicious,' said Ahalya.

5

It was one in the morning. Doctor Sahib was having a terrifying dream.

Suddenly, Ahalya came and said, 'Please come and have a look at what's happening to Jagiya. It looks like her tongue has gone stiff. She doesn't say a thing. Her eyes have glazed over.'

The doctor sat up with a start. He peered around for a moment, as if wondering if this too were a dream. Then he said, 'What did you say? What's happened to Jagiya?'

Ahalya described Jagiya's condition again. A faint smile appeared on the doctor's face.

He said, 'The thief has been caught. The spell has done its work.'

'And what if it was someone from the family who'd taken it?'

'Then they'd be in the same state, they'd learn a lesson for life.'

'You'd kill in pursuit of five hundred rupees?'

'Not for five hundred rupees—if need be I can spend five thousand—but just as penalty for deception.'

'You're so heartless.'

'If I cover you in gold from head to foot, you'll start thinking of me as an angel of goodness, won't you? I'm so sorry I couldn't take this testimonial from you.'

Saying this, he went into Jagiya's room. Her condition was far worse than what Ahalya had described. There was death shadowing her face, her hands and feet had stiffened, and there was no sign of a pulse. His mother was repeatedly splashing water on Jagiya's face to bring her back to her senses. The doctor was shocked at her condition. He ought to have been pleased with the success of his remedy. Jagiya had stolen the money so there was no need for any more proof. But he had no idea that a spell could work its effect so quickly and was so murderous. He'd wanted to see the thief go down on his knees and moan in agony. His desire for revenge was being more than fulfilled and yet it was a bitter morsel to swallow. Instead of feeling happy, the tragic scene wounded him. In arrogance we exaggerate the extent of our heartlessness and cruelty. What eventually happens is so much more consequential than we think. The idea of the battlefield can be so poetic; the poetry of the battle cry can generate so much heat in us. But seeing the scattered limbs of the crushed corpse, which man does not shudder? Pity is man's natural virtue.

Apart from this, he had no idea that a frail soul like Jagiya's would be sacrificed for his rage. He had believed that the blow of his revenge would fall on some spirited person; he even considered his wife and son deserving of this blow. But to kill the dead, to trample on the trampled? He felt this contrary to his natural inclination. This action of Jagiya's should have been forgiven. One who scrabbled for bread, longed for clothes, the house of whose desires was always dark, whose wishes had never been fulfilled—it's not surprising if such a person is tempted. He immediately went into the pharmacy, mixed into a new blend all the best medicines effective for reviving a person and poured it down Jagiya's throat. It had no effect. He brought out a defibrillator and tried bringing her back to consciousness with the help of that. In a little while her eyes opened.

Looking at the doctor with a scared face, the way a boy looks at his teacher's stick, she said in a wan voice, 'Hai Ram, my liver is on fire, take your money, there's a pot in the alcove, that's where it is. Don't roast me on coals. I stole this money to go on pilgrimage. Don't you have any pity, setting me on fire for a handful of rupees? I didn't think you such a blackguard. Hai Ram.'

Saying this she fainted again, her pulse died, her lips turned blue and her limbs stiffened.

Looking at Ahalya meekly, the doctor said, 'I've done whatever I could, it's beyond me now to revive her. How did I know that this accursed spell is so destructive? If it happens to kill her, I'll have to repent all my life. I'll never be free of the knocks of conscience. What should I do, my mind isn't working.'

'Call the civil surgeon, perhaps he can give her some good medicine. One shouldn't knowingly push someone else into the fire.'

'The civil surgeon can't do much more than what I've already done. Her condition is worsening every moment. God knows what mantra that murderer said. His mother kept trying to convince me but in my anger I didn't pay her any attention.'

His mother said, 'Son, call the one who's put the curse. What to do? If she dies, her murder will be on our heads. She'll torment the family forever.'

6

It was almost two in the morning; a cold wind pricked the bones. The doctor took long strides towards Budh Chaudhuri's. He looked around uselessly for an ekka or tonga. Budh's house appeared to be a long way off. He kept feeling that he'd lost his way. *I've come this way often, I've never passed this garden, or seen this letterbox by the road, and the bridge was by no means there. I'm definitely lost. Who should I ask?* He was annoyed at his memory and ran in the same direction for a while. *Who knows if that wretch will be around at this hour, he must be lying in a drunken stupor. And what if, back home, the poor thing has passed away?* He often thought of turning in some other direction but his inner voice didn't let him move from the straight path.

Soon, Budh's house could be seen. Doctor Sahib breathed a sigh of relief. He went to the door and banged the latch hard. From inside a dog answered raucously but no human word was heard. He banged the door harder and the dog became louder; the old lady woke up.

She said, 'Who is breaking down the door so late in the night?'

'It's me, I was here a little while ago.'

The old lady recognized the voice; she understood that some calamity had befallen someone in the family, otherwise why would he come so late. But Budh hadn't cast the spell yet, how had it taken effect? When she had tried to reason he wouldn't listen. Now they were properly caught. She got up, lit an oil lamp and came out with it.

'Is Budh Chaudhuri asleep? Please can you wake him?' asked Doctor Sahib.

'No, Babuji, I won't wake him at this hour, he'll eat me alive. Even if the Lord Sahib came to see him at night, he wouldn't get up.'

Doctor Sahib explained the situation briefly and implored her to wake Budh.

Budh came out on his own, and rubbing his eyes, said, 'Tell me, Babuji, what's your command?'

Irritated, the old woman said, 'How come your sleep broke today? If I'd tried to wake you you'd have set upon me.'

The doctor said, 'I've explained the situation to the old lady, you can ask her.'

'Nothing,' said the old lady. 'You put the curse, his servant had taken the money and is now about to die.'

'The poor woman is dying. Do something to save her!' said the doctor.

'That's a bad thing you're telling me. Turning back a curse is not easy,' said Budh.

'Son, one's life is at risk, don't you know? If the curse happens to fall on the one who reverses it, then it might be difficult to survive,' said his mother.

'She can only be saved if you save her, please oblige me.'

'For the sake of another's life, should one throw away one's own?' asked the old woman.

The doctor said, 'You do this work day and night, you know all the tricks. You can kill and you can bring to life. I never believed in these things but seeing the miracle you pulled off I'm left dumbfounded. You've benefited so many people, take pity on that poor old woman.'

Budh seemed to be melting a little, but his mother was much cleverer than him in matters of business. She was afraid he would soften and mess things up. She didn't give Budh a chance to say anything.

She said, 'That is all very well but we have children too. We don't know which way things will go. It will come down on our heads, won't it? Once your purpose is met you'll move aside. It's not a laughing matter to reverse a spell.'

'Yes, Babuji, it's a very risky job.'

'If it's a very risky job I don't want it done for free, do I?'

'How much will you give, fifty or hundred at the most? How long can we live on that?' said the old woman. 'Reversing a spell is putting one's hand in a snake-hole, jumping into fire. Only by God's grace can a life be saved.'

'So, mother, I am with you. Say whatever you want. I just have to save that poor woman's life. We're losing time on talk here and I don't know what her condition is like there.'

The old woman said, 'You're the one who's wasting time. You decide the matter and then he'll go with you. For your sake I'm taking this danger on my head, if it was anyone else I'd refuse outright. I'm drinking poison knowingly, doing you this favour.'

Every second felt as long as a year to Doctor Sahib. He wanted to take Budh with him right away. If she died, what would he mend when he got there? Money was of no account to him at that moment. He was only concerned that Jagiya be saved from the jaws of death. The frenzy of pity had made absolutely insignificant the money for which he used to sacrifice his own necessities and his wife's desires.

He said, 'You tell me, what can I say, but whatever you want to say, say quickly.'

The old woman said, 'Okay, then give us five hundred rupees, the work can't be done for less.'

Budh, looked at his mother in surprise, and Doctor Sahib felt faint. Dejectedly, he said, 'That is beyond my capacity. It seems she's fated to die.'

'Let it be then,' said the old woman. 'It's not as if we're burdened by our lives. We took on the responsibility of this work because of your entreaties. Go back to sleep, Budh.'

'Old mother, don't be so cruel, only man comes to the help of man.'

Budh said, 'No, Babuji, I'm prepared in every way to do your work. She said five hundred, you reduce it a bit. But yes, keep the danger in mind.'

The old woman said, 'Why don't you go and sleep? If money is dear to him, isn't your life dear to you? If tomorrow you start spitting blood then nothing can be done. Who will you leave your children to? Do you have anything in the house?'

Hesitating, Doctor Sahib said two hundred and fifty rupees. Budh agreed, the matter was settled, the doctor and he set out for his house. He had never experienced such spiritual happiness before. The man who goes to court and returns having won the lost case could not be happier. He went along with a bounce in his step and kept telling Budh to walk faster. When they got home they found Jagiya at the brink of death. It appeared that her every breath would be her last. His mother and wife were both sitting tearful and hopeless. They gave Budh a desolate look. Doctor Sahib couldn't stop his tears either. When he bent towards Jagiya a teardrop fell on her withered, yellow face.

The situation had made Budh alert. Putting his hand on the old woman's body, he said, 'Babuji, I can't do a thing now, she's dying.'

Doctor Sahib said entreatingly, 'No, Chaudhuri, for God's sake start your mantra. If her life is saved, I'll remain your slave for life.'

'You're asking me to deliberately eat poison. I didn't realize that the gods of the spell were so angry right now. They're sitting inside me and saying, if you snatch away our victim we'll swallow you.'

'Get the gods to come around somehow,' said the doctor.

'It's very difficult to get them to come around. Give me five hundred rupees, then she'll be saved. I'll have to exert great effort to bring down the curse.'

'If I give you five hundred rupees, will you save her life?'

'Yes, I promise.'

Doctor Sahib went like lightning into his room and, returning with a purse of five hundred rupees, placed it before Budh. Budh looked at the purse victoriously. Then he put Jagiya's head in his lap and began moving his hand over it. He would mutter something and say, 'Chhoo, chhoo.' For a second his face became scary and what looked like flames leapt from it. He began to writhe repeatedly. In this condition he sang a song off-key, but his hand remained on Jagiya's head. At last, after half an hour, like a dying lamp that has been replenished with oil, Jagiya's eyes opened. Her condition improved slowly. A crow's cawing was heard and she turned over and sat up.

7

It was seven o'clock and Jagiya was in a sweet slumber. She looked well. Budh had just left with the money. Doctor

Sahib's mother said, 'Before we knew what was happening, he took off with five hundred rupees.'

The doctor said, 'Why don't you say that he brought the dead to life? Is her life not worth even that much?'

'Check if there are five hundred rupees in the alcove or not.'

'No, don't touch that money, let it stay there. She'd taken it to go on pilgrimage, it'll go towards that end alone.'

'All this money was in her fate only.'

'Only five hundred was in her fate, the rest was in mine. Thanks to it I learnt a lesson I won't forget all my life. You won't find me tight-fisted over the necessary things any more.'

Translated from the Hindi by Anjum Hasan

A Dhobi's Honour

1

Bechu Dhobi loved his home and village as much as every man did. He ate simply, often barely half his fill, but his village was still far more precious to him than the whole world. Though he had to suffer the abuses of the old peasant women, the honour of being called Bechu Dada by the young wives was also his. He was always invited to every occasion of joy or grief; especially at weddings, his presence was no less essential than that of the bride and the groom themselves. His wife would be ceremonially worshipped inside the house; he would be welcomed graciously at the doorstep. Wearing *peshwaz*, bells tied to his waist, one hand beating the mridang, one hand on his ear, when he would lustily sing the traditional *viraha* and *bol* extempore, along with the troupe of singers and musicians, his eyes would glaze over with pride. Yes, Bechu was quite content with his lot as a washerman. But sometimes, when the atrocities of the zamindar's men became unbearable, he would long to run away from the village.

Karinda Sahib had four or five peons. Each of them had large families. Bechu had to wash all their clothes for free.

He did not have an iron. To iron their clothes he had to beg and plead with the dhobis of other villages. If he ever took back the clothes unironed, he would have to face hell for it. He would be thrashed, have to stand for hours in front of the *chaupal*, and such abuses would rain down on him that passers-by would cover their ears and women would lower their heads in shame.

It was the month of Jeth. All the nearby ponds and lakes had dried up. Bechu would have to leave for a distant lake while it was still dark. Even there, the dhobis already had their slots fixed. Bechu's slot fell on the fifth day. He would load his bundle of washing and arrive there long before dawn. But it was not possible to stand in that scorching Jeth sun beyond nine or ten. Even half the load wouldn't get washed. He would bundle up the unwashed clothes and return home. The simple village folk would listen to his story of woe and quieten down; they would neither abuse him nor beat him up. They too had to work the plough and hoe the fields in that fierce Jeth sun. The soles of their feet, too, were cracked and sore; they knew his pain. But it wasn't so easy to please Karinda Sahib. His men would forever be standing on Bechu's head. 'You don't bring the clothes for eight-eight days on end,' they would say grimly. 'Is this winter or what? Clothes get grimy and smelly with sweat in a day here, and it makes no difference to you.' Bechu would fold over himself, beg, plead and somehow manage to pacify them.

Once, nine days passed, and their clothes were still not ready. They had been washed but not yet ironed. Finally, helpless, Bechu reached the zamindar's chaupal with the clothes on the tenth day. Fear had frozen his limbs. As soon as Karinda Sahib saw him, he went red with rage. 'Why, you rascal, do you want to live in this village or not?'

Bechu put the bundle of clothes down on the wooden platform and said, 'What to do, Sarkar, there's no water anywhere—and neither do I have an iron.'

Karinda: 'Everyone in the world has water except you. There's no cure left for you except to throw you out of the village. Scoundrel! Fooling the midwife with a bloated stomach—no water, no iron indeed!'

Bechu: 'Malik, the whole village is yours; if it pleases you, let me stay, if it pleases you, throw me out, but don't taint me with this accusation. That is a custom common to city dhobis. I have spent a lifetime serving you. But whatever the mistakes and lapses may have been on my part, my intentions have never been bad. If anyone in the village says that I have done such a thing, I will accept my fault.'

It is futile to try and reason with a tyrant. Karinda Sahib abused and cursed him some more. Bechu too pleaded and swore in the name of justice and mercy. The result was that he had to consume turmeric and jaggery for eight days to relieve the pain of the thrashing he received. On the ninth day, somehow or the other, he washed the remaining clothes, collected his belongings and, without a word to anyone, left for Patna in the night. He was deprived of the fortitude necessary to take leave of one's old customers.

2

When Bechu arrived in the city, it was as if there was already an empty space waiting for him. He only had to take up a room on rent, and things started falling into place. At first he nearly fainted on hearing how much the rent was. In the village, he wouldn't even get this much for a month's washing. But when he learnt the rates for washing here, the rent didn't bite so much. In just one month he had more customers than he could count. There was no dearth of water. He was true to his word, and still free of the ills of city life. Sometimes, the earnings of a single day would exceed what he'd earn in a year back home in the village.

But in just three or four months, the ways of the city began to influence him. Earlier, he used to drink coconut water. Now, he got a bubbly hookah. His feet, once bare, were attired in shoes, and the unpolished grain he was accustomed to began to cause indigestion. Earlier, once in a while, on some festive occasion, he would have a little liquor. Now, to beat exhaustion, he started drinking every day. His wife acquired a taste for ornaments—'The other *dhobin*s go about all dressed up here, am I any less than them?' she would say. His boys would get excited every time a peddler came by hawking his wares and run out as soon as they heard '*Moongfali!* Halva!'

Meanwhile, the landlord raised the rent. Even straw and oil cakes were as dear as pearls here. A good bit of his earnings went into feeding the two bulls that carried his load of dirty clothes for washing. So whatever he would have managed to save over several months earlier now vanished. Sometimes, the expenses would mount higher than his earnings, but no means of thrift would come to mind. Eventually, his wife started whisking away his customers' clothes and renting them out to others on the sly. When Bechu came to know, he was furious. 'If I hear one more complaint, there'll be no one worse than me! It was this accusation that forced me to leave the village of my forefathers. Do you want us to be banished from here as well?'

His wife answered, 'But it is you who can't do without liquor for even a day. Do I get the money to blow up on myself? And yes, leave something for household expenses before you go, I'm not getting any sweets out of this.'

But gradually, the matter of ethics began to bow its head before necessity. Once, Bechu lay ill with fever for many days. His wife took him to the vaid in a palanquin. The vaid wrote down a prescription. There was no money in the house. Bechu looked at his wife with desperate eyes and asked, 'What now? Must the medicine be bought?'

'I'll do as you say.'

'Can't you borrow from someone?'

'I've borrowed from everyone I could; it's become difficult to walk in the mohalla nowadays. Whom to ask now? What work I can do myself, I do. I can't cut myself up into pieces and die, can I? A little extra money used to come in, but you put a stop to that too. So what say do I have then? The bulls have been hungry for two days. If I get two rupees, I could feed them.'

'Fine, do what you wish, but make do somehow. I have now learnt—an honest man cannot make a living in the city.'

From that day on, the ways of other city washermen were followed in his house.

3

A lawyer's cleric, Munshi Dataram, lived in Bechu's neighbourhood. Sometimes, during a break, Bechu would go sit with him. It was a matter between neighbours, so no accounts were kept for his washing. Munshiji would always receive Bechu graciously, hand him his chillum to smoke, and if some delicacy had been made at his place, he would have it sent for Bechu's boys. But yes, he would make sure that these little gestures did not exceed the cost of the washing.

It was summer, the season of marriages. Munshiji had to go for a wedding. He got a long pipe made for his hookah, bought a well-oiled chillum and pointed-toe *salimshahi* shoes, and borrowed a rug from his lawyer sahib and a gold ring and buttons from his friend. He didn't have much difficulty procuring all these things. But he was embarrassed to borrow clothes for the wedding. There was no scope for getting new ones stitched. It was no easy matter to get made-to-order breast-pocketed kurtas, silk achkans, tight-ringed *chunnatdaar nainsukh* pyjamas and a Benarasi turban. These items would cost a handsome amount. Buying silk-bordered dhotis and a shawl of Kashi silk was also no trivial matter. He kept worrying about all this for days. In the end, he could think of no one other than Bechu to bail him out.

When Bechu came and sat by him in the evening, Munshiji humbly said, 'Bechu, I have to attend a wedding. I have managed to collect everything else I need, but getting new clothes made is a problem. Money is not a concern; by your good wishes these hands are never empty. The profession is also such that no matter what fee you ask for, it is less; some poor fool or another with a fat purse is always there to fleece. But you know the rush of weddings these days—tailors don't have a moment's respite, they charge twice the normal rates, and even then they make you wait for months. If you have any clothes suitable for me, I'll just borrow them for two or three days and somehow get it over and done with. What does

A Dhobi's Honour

it cost anyone to give an invitation? At the most, they might get it printed. But why don't people ever consider the fact that the invitees too have to make preparations, overcome so many difficulties? If there was a custom in one's community that he who sends an invitation must also be the one who arranges for everything necessary for the invitees to attend, then people wouldn't send out these marriage invitations so thoughtlessly. So tell me, you'll help me out, won't you, Bechu?'

Out of obligation, Bechu said, 'Munshiji, how can I ever refuse you? But the thing is that there are so many weddings these days that customers are also getting impatient for their clothes and sending for them two or three times a day. It shouldn't happen that while I give you the clothes here, the owner shows up at the door asking for them.'

Munshiji answered, 'What's the big deal in delaying delivery for two or three days? You could easily delay them for weeks if you wished—not put them through the furnace yet, not ironed them yet, the washing ghats are shut—you don't have any dearth of excuses. Won't you even do this much for your neighbour?'

'No, Munshiji, I would give my life for you. Come and choose your clothes so I can run the iron over them once more and make them fresh. At worst, I'll have to hear the abuses of my customers. So even if I do lose a couple, that's nothing to mope about.'

4

Munshiji reached the wedding in style. His Benarasi turban, silk achkan, long coat and shawl created such an impression that people thought he was some wealthy nobleman. Munshiji took Bechu along with him, and made sure he was taken care of. He got him a bottle of liquor and a plate of food when he went in to eat. He would keep calling him Choudhury instead of Bechu. After all, this pomp and show was all thanks to him.

It was past midnight. The revelry and celebrations were over, and people were preparing to retire for the night. Bechu was lying next to Munshiji's cot under a sheet. Munshiji took off his clothes and carefully hung them on a line. The hookah was ready. As he lay down and began to smoke, an atai from the troupe of musicians accompanying the wedding party suddenly came and stood before him, and asked, 'May I ask you where you got this achkan and turban from, sir?'

Munshiji looked at him suspiciously and said, 'What does that mean?'

'It means that both of these belong to me.'

Munshiji then somewhat recklessly ventured to say, 'So in your opinion, no one can possess a silk coat and turban other than you?'

'Why not? He whom Allah gives to wears it. There are so many of them here, each greater than the last. I hardly come in that reckoning. But both *these* things are mine. If you can find another man in this city who possesses the same achkan, I'll pay you whatever you ask. There's no other craftsman in the whole city like him. He cuts clothes with such finesse that one could kiss his hands. My insignia is on the turban—I can show you if you bring it here. All I want to ask is where did you procure these garments from.'

Munshiji realized that this was not the place to argue. If things got out of hand, it could be humiliating. Diplomacy

A Dhobi's Honour

wouldn't work here. So he said humbly, 'Bhai, do not ask me that; this is not the time or place to tell you these things. Your honour and mine are one and the same. Just think that this is the way the world goes around. If I had to get such clothes made, I would have spent thousands right now. I just had to attend the wedding somehow, that is all. Your clothes will not get spoiled, I take full responsibility. I'll take better care of them than if they were mine.'

'I'm not concerned about the clothes. By your grace, Allah has given me plenty. May He protect the rich; thanks be to Him, all five fingers are immersed in ghee. And neither do I wish to malign your good name. I am a slave at your feet. All I want to know is who gave you these clothes. I had given them to Bechu Dhobi to wash. So is it that some thief whisked them away from Bechu's house, or did some other dhobi steal them from him and give them to you? Because Bechu certainly would not have given these clothes to you with his own hands. He does not do such things. In fact, *I* too had wanted to make such an arrangement with him once. I even put money into his hands. But, sahib, he picked up the money and threw it away, and he gave me such a talking-to that I was stunned out of my wits. I don't know what the understanding is here, because thereafter I've never even mentioned something like that to him. But I find it hard to believe he has stooped so low. That is why I ask you again and again, from where did you get these clothes?'

'Your surmise about Bechu is absolutely right. He is indeed a selfless man. But neighbours also have some rights. He lives in my neighbourhood, we are part of each other's lives. He saw my need, and gave in. *Bas.* That is all. And I would do the same for him.'

The atai had neither put money into Bechu's hands, nor had Bechu given him a talking-to. The atai had exaggerated Bechu's selflessness. But this little exaggeration had a far greater impact on Bechu than if he had merely spoken the truth. Bechu was not asleep. He had heard every word the atai had spoken. He felt as if his soul had just awoken from a deep sleep. *The world sees me as such an honest, true and deceitless man. And I . . . I am such a fraud and a cheat. It was on this false charge that I left the village of my forefathers. But after coming here, I've got ruined running after liquor, ghee and sugar.*

5

Six months passed by. It was evening. Some guests had arrived to discuss Bechu's son Malkhan's marriage. When Bechu came in to talk to his wife about something, she said, 'Where will the liquor come from? Do you have some money?'

Bechu: 'Didn't I already give you whatever I had?'

Wife: 'But I bought rice, dal, and ghee with that. I've cooked for seven people. All of it got used up.'

Bechu: 'So what do I do then?'

Wife: 'They will hardly eat without drinking first. It will be so embarrassing.'

Bechu: 'Whether it is embarrassing or disgraceful, it is not possible for me to get liquor now. At the most what will happen? The marriage will not be fixed. So let it not.'

Wife: 'Hasn't that shawl come in for washing? Go pawn it at a bania's shop and get back four or five rupees. You can retrieve it in two or three days. We must keep our honour.

Or else, everyone will say, "All talk, and nothing to show. He couldn't even serve us liquor."'

Bechu: 'What are you saying? Is this *dushala* mine to pawn?'

Wife: 'Whosoever's it may be, at this moment, just use it. No one will come to know.'

Bechu: 'No, this I cannot do, whether we get liquor or not.'

And he walked out. When he came in again, he saw his wife digging up something from a hole in the ground. Seeing him, she quickly covered the hole with the end of her sari.

Bechu went out again smiling to himself.

Translated from the Hindi by Moyna Mazumdar

Notes

Thakur's Well

First published in Hindi as 'Thakur ka Kuan' in *Jagaran* (August 1932), and later collected in *Mansarovar* 1 (1936). Not available in Urdu. Transliterated from Hindi to Urdu for *Kulliyaat-e Premchand* 13 (2003).

Salvation

First published in Hindi with the title 'Sadgati' in *Vishaal Bharat* (October 1931), and later included in *Mansarovar* 4 (1939). In Urdu, it was published in *Aakhiri Tohfa* (1934) with the title 'Nijaat'. Now available in *Kulliyaat-e Premchand* 13 (2003).

Temple

First published as 'Mandir' in the Hindi monthly *Chand* (May 1927), and subsequently included in *Mansarovar* 5

(1946). In Urdu it was published in *Prem Chaleesi* 1 (1930) with the same title. Now available in *Kulliyaat-e Premchand* 12 (2003).

One and a Quarter Ser of Wheat

First published in Urdu as 'Sawa Ser Gehun' in Chand (November, 1924), and later included in Firdaus-e Khayaal (1929). Now available in Kulliyaat-e Premchand 11 (2001). It is available in Hindi in Mansarovar 4 (1939).

The Woman Who Sold Grass

First published in Hindi as 'Ghaaswali' in *Madhuri* (December 1929), and later included in *Mansarovar* 1 (1936). In Urdu, it was published with the same title in *Prem Chaleesi* 2 (1930). Now available in *Kulliyaat-e Premchand* 13 (2003).

The Mantra

First published in Hindi as 'Mantra' in Madhuri (February 1926), and later included in Mansarovar 5 (1946). In Urdu, it was included in the volume Khaak-e-Parwana (1928) with the title 'Taalif'. Now available in Kulliyaat-e Premchand 12 (2003).

The Lashes of Good Fortune

First published in Hindi as 'Saubhagya ke Kodey' in Prabha (June 1924), and later included in Mansarovar 3 (1938). In Urdu, it was included as 'Nekbakhti ke Tazianey' in Firdaus-e

Khayaal (1929). Now available in Kulliyaat-e Premchand 11 (2001).

From Both Sides

First published in Urdu as 'Dono Taraf Se' in *Zamana* (March 1911). Now available in *Kulliyaat-e Premchand* 9 (2000). It was published in Hindi as 'Dono Taraf Se' in *Naya Prateek* (October 1976), and collected in *Premchand ka Aprapya Sahitya* 1 (1988).

Witchcraft

First published in Hindi with the title 'Mooth' in *Maryada* (January 1922), and later collected in *Prem Pacheesi* (1923) and *Mansarovar* 8 (1950). It was published in Urdu with the same title in *Zamana* (December 1922), and later collected in *Khwab-o Khayal* (1928). Now available in *Kulliyaat-e Premchand* 11 (2001).

A Dhobi's Honour

First published in Urdu as 'Husn-e Zan' in *Zamana* (October 1922), and collected much later in *Kulliyaat-e Premchand* 11 (2001). In Hindi, it is included in *Mansarovar* 7 (1947) as 'Lokmat ka Samman'.

Note on Translators

Shaheen Saba is a PhD student of English at Jamia Millia Islamia, New Delhi.

Ranjeeta Dutta has completed an MPhil in English from Jamia Millia Islamia, New Delhi.

Anjum Hasan is the author of the novels *The Cosmopolitans*, *Neti, Neti* and *Lunatic in My Head*. She has also published a collection of stories, *Difficult Pleasures*, and a book of poems, *Street on the Hill*. Her books have been nominated for various awards.

Vikas Jain teaches English at Zakir Husain Delhi College (Evening), Delhi University.

Meenakshi F. Paul is a faculty member in the Department of English at Himachal Pradesh University. She is a translator and poet. She has published several articles and books, including a volume on bilingual poetry, *Kindling from the*

Terraced Fields, and a book of translation, *Short Stories of Himachal Pradesh*.

Moyna Mazumdar has worked with several publishing houses as editor. She also translates from Hindi and Bengali into English.